Here is How it Happens

Ampersand Books
St. Petersburg, FL
www.ampersand-books.com

*This is a work of fiction.
Names and characters are either the product of the
author's imagination or are used fictitiously.
All resemblances to any person, living or dead, are entirely coincidental.*

Copyright © 2011 Spencer Dew

*All rights reserved. No part of this book may be reproduced by any means,
except for short excerpts for review or academic purposes, without the
express written consent of the publisher.*

Published 2013 Ampersand Books
First Edition
ISBN 978-0-9841025-9-4

Cover design by Matthew Revert
Layout by Pequod Book Design

Here is How it Happens
Spencer Dew

AMPERSAND BOOKS

Florida

Autumn descends on Northern Ohio.

Here is how it happens:

With the sky split into layers of fiery late-afternoon light and clouds like lava over the hills, the melodrama of nature consumes the landscape.

The valleys beyond us blaze in amber and gold, a scene identical to the postcards in the rack by the cash register, ten cents apiece, three for a quarter.

There is a glint against the glass of the restaurant window, white light on fingerprints and greasy smears, a dried trail of ketchup.

But you are unfazed.

You squint toward the sun, the fringe along your jacket's arms slapping as you pack your cigarettes against your palm.

You say, "Anesthesia."

And you sigh, as if this were the last thing, sinking your reserves into a single act, to convey meaning through breath alone.

"But isn't it kind of early to start worrying about something like that," I say. "I mean, she just *conceived*, right?"

"That's what I'm saying, kiddo. This early on and already talk of surgical removal, c-section, whatever the butchers call it. *Cesarean*.

"There's risk involved. I know how it is. People don't come back, or they come back changed."

You drag the candle over to your side of the booth, hold back your hair as you lean over the red glass dome and light your cigarette.

"But Courtney," I say. "I mean, maybe, all things considered, you're being a bit extreme."

"The whole process is extreme, Martin. A gamble with death. Nine months of severe anxiety, nausea, and pain.

"When you stop to think of it up real close, all the possible complications, it's a wonder anyone makes it out alive.

"Just puts things in perspective. That's all I'm saying. That we're here," you say, "And whole. Consider the variables.

"We exist against innumerable odds. I haven't even mentioned birth defects. I haven't even used the word 'disease'."

Dead leaves spin in circles across the parking lot, piling into a thick drift against the walls of the swimming pool, the construction site of the new Holiday Inn.

Across the highway, a flock of large, black birds gathers around a piece of roadkill on the gravel in front of the feed store.

A kitten, perhaps. A puppy. A household pet. Somewhere, a child is walking along a ditch, calling out in singsong.

"Cholera," you say, "Rickets, shingles, botulism, gonococcus, sickle cell anemia. We're hemmed round, kiddo. Metastasizing carcinomas."

You spread the words like butter over hot meat, pausing only to pull fire toward your lungs.

"Strep," I say.

"Strep," you say.

You smile, infection passing as a private joke.

Embers of sunset wash over you, erasing the lines under your eyes, brightening the bleached streaks in your hair. The light sparks off the guitar strings wrapped around your wrist.

"And these are only long-range options," you say. "Last Sunday's *Plain Dealer* had a piece about a miscarriage found in a toilet at the science museum.

"Chilly, blue stillbirth—To pass something that large and dead from your body, I mean, it has to take something of you with it."

A pickup pulls into the lot of the feed store, scattering the ravens into the sky. Whatever they were eating, the truck rolls right over it, parks on the corpse.

You say, "Tegan was telling me about this show she saw once, some cable thing on tropical disease, how sometimes babies are born without skin. They just pop out, right, and no skin, just bloody, screaming, writhing monsters. And the air burns them, and they vomit and shit and generally turn themselves into puddles on the delivery room floor.

"But that's death by exposure, just like the rest of us, right? Which is why I can say *monsters*, right? Because they are born, and they breathe, register sensation, respond to pain.

"So much depends on this technical distinction: It's nothing more than tissue till it screams."

***

Outside the windows of this restaurant, our childhoods are rotting away.

Autumn after autumn finding us older, weary, closer to some kind of end. Conspiracies of circumstance closing in around us, due dates and deadlines, dry chalk dust and bonfire winds.

The cold is sneaking in already, spreading sharp and quick as a shadow across a neck, the perpetual promise that each winter will be worse than the last.

All that is green will turn to brown. All that is blue will turn to gray. The months to come will be barren, glacial, and dark.

This is the grinding cycle that marks our lives: The ceiling fan above us turns with a tap, tap, tap, and the waitress refills our coffees.

"And that was just half of it," you say. "As soon as I hung up with my aunt—which was pretty much right after I tried to suggest that maybe during the whole pregnancy thing she should at least switch to filters and start diluting her whiskey with something more substantial than ice—as soon as I hung up with her, the phone rings again."

"Sloan?"

"Of course, Sloan. Sloan, Sloan, Sloan. Remember being a kid, saying the same word over and over until it stopped making any sense, just became a blur of sound, a string of incomprehensible syllables, and then you'd get scared, like maybe one day you'd forget all words, like your whole conception of reality through language could just go away, and all you could do would be to sit in the corner and beat your head against the wall?

"Well, it's like that with Sloan sometimes. He'd been waiting on the phone, he said, just listening to the busy signal. 'Babe, babe, I didn't expect a voice', he said.

"He was a little bit confused, but the gist of it is that he's borrowed somebody's van, and he says he's going to come down here tomorrow.

"And now—I mean, he's never been here, kiddo. Not once. Not at all. Not ever. I go home all the time, every weekend some times, and he's *never* come, not to help me move in last year, not this year, not after any of the holidays, not when strep hit last spring. He doesn't have a car, sure, but he doesn't go to school, and he doesn't have a job, and there is no reason for *anyone* to stay in Niles all the time."

"I see Sloan as the kind of guy who develops a symbiotic relationship with his couch," I say.

"Yeah, yeah. And with his TV and his roach clip and his stupid video racing game, but what about me?"

"So he's finally coming," I say. "Why isn't this a good thing?"

You concentrate on your cigarette. You draw heat toward your heart.

"I'm close here, Martin. I'm almost saying something, something of relevance for us both.

"Sometimes we do things just to torture ourselves. Sometimes we have faith only because we know we do not believe."

You mouth the words again, silent. "That's good, huh? I should write that one down."

I say, "Faith is a bit clichéd."

"Oh, that's even better. 'Faith is a bit clichéd.'"

* * *

The air is thick with tobacco, heavy with the smells of sausage and syrup. Silverware scrapes against cheap china as all around us calloused men and women hunch over their twenty-four-hour breakfast skillets.

The Mennonite girls lean the edges of their bonnets close together, whisper and giggle.

The trucker in the corner booth runs his palm down the crease of a newspaper, shifts his weight and hisses out a long fart.

The retarded woman at the center table just stares at you, drooling chunks of half-chewed biscuit, cream gravy.

Beams of sunlight catch in the smoke, smoldering, hazy, streaming across the restaurant, the coat racks, Carhartt jackets and hats advertising herbicide, farm equipment.

And the colors cry over the hills.

And the sunset looks like a plane crash, like a horrible disaster.

A storm of blood light, clotting solid in the sky, a sunset that threatens to go on forever, till the man in the John Deere cap stands and begins to close the blinds.

I pour sugar into my coffee. A shade rattles behind my shoulder, and the sun disappears like the sugar rasping out of the jar's trapdoor hole.

You shake pepper over the remnants of your eggs, then unfold your napkin and cover your plate.

The retarded woman begins to moan.

"So, you're right. I don't want him to come. I mean, I'm not *sure*. I guess I know that I really don't want him to come because he'll be difficult and out of place, and he's never met anybody, and he's real jealous, and he hates you already, and everyone will hate him, and I'll be the one who ends up feeling like shit, and I can't stress enough just how not very smart he is.

"But. I mean, he's never come here. And I *love* him, you know. So I got some pretty violent ambivalence going on here."

I say, "Maybe, all things considered, you and he are not the model of a healthy relationship."

You say, "Healthy relationships are a bit clichéd, don't you think?"

You wedge your cigarette in a groove of the ashtray, and it smolders there as the sunset presses against the windows, an infernal glow against the slats of the shades.

Red, red, red. It could be hell outside this restaurant, angels wrestling in the parking lot of the feed store.

Best to remain calm, take comfort in blind routine: The waitress removes our plates, refills our coffees with her free hand. There is no decaf here.

I say, "Padhya came out here with me once, one weekend when she drove down from Cleveland so we could argue in person and have really angry and frustrating sex."

"She hated it, right?"

"It's hard to tell with the sex anymore."

"I mean this place, kiddo. She hated the Amish Kitchen."

"She did. *Common*, that was the word she used."

"Great head for words, that little pre-med of yours."

"Immunology. It's different from pre-med. Less human contact involved."

"Not big on bedside manner, that little immunologist of yours." You smile. You smoke your cigarette. You say, "What did she order?"

"She didn't. Well, she had a cup of tea, then we drove back to town."

"A cup of tea. And you ate at Steak Emporium?"

"Yeah. We drove back and ate at Steak Emporium. Then, if I'm remembering correctly, that was one of the nights I pretended to sleep so we wouldn't have to make love. She sat at my desk and did calculus homework, played solitaire on her laptop."

You grind out your cigarette, pushing the butt across the ashtray in a five-pointed star.

You say, "I used to think that once the conversation and companionship and sex all fell through, a relationship would just collapse. And I used to think that the word collapse implied *not going on*."

"There's the comfort of the familiar. Security."

"With Sloan, everything is routine. Familiar is too kind a word. Our conversations sound rehearsed. We shuttle through the same dumb sexual choreography like it's just a chore we have to perform in order to smoke cigarettes in bed. I come when he leaves the room, and I think he comes playing that stupid racing game.

"But the worst part is that when we have nothing else to say to each other, which is the constant, we just fill the silence by exchanging clumsy confessions of love. Love: The all-purpose conversation filler."

The sizzle of pork fat. The creek of bar stools at the counter. The drone of the ceiling fans stirring the smoke.

One of the cooks comes through the swinging doors from the kitchen with a fresh pie. He slides it into the back of the glass pie case, next to the cash register, above the larger display case for fresh breads, jams, jellies, preserves.

Behind all this, on the half-wall of the kitchen, there's a mural of Ohio history. Painted by one of the college's art professors back in the seventies, the mural lays out the whole sordid saga of our state, tourist hokum counterbalanced with social-realist macabre.

Above the fat flannel back of some guy sitting at the counter I can make out the top of a buckeye tree, the S Bridge on the National Road, a sheaf of wheat, a bundle of arrows, and a heroic-size tableau of Mad Anthony Wayne braining some vicious Indian bastard with the butt of his rifle.

This is the heart of it all.

We come to the Amish Kitchen to get wired, and we come to the Amish Kitchen to calm down after being wired too long.

We come here to avoid the cafeteria, to drown in and further stylize our still-developing artifice, to feel *real*, like people who *need* steel toes in their boots.

Your face framed by the columns of steam rising from our coffee mugs, a rough halo of other people's smoke, you pick at your fingernails, chip off a little more black polish from your thumb. You twist your hand around, check your watch.

"Well, we've kept her waiting forty-five minutes. Might as well make it an even hour."

"Maybe she found another way back to campus," I say.

"This is Kim we're talking about, kiddo. She's still out there, snagging her nylons on the yard art, polishing off the day's second volume of prose poems, her second series of watercolor sketches."

"Sometimes I think she's not so bad," I say. "But she is, huh?"

"Our situations could be worse," you say. "We could have been born Kim Reese."

"You heard about the extra three thousand she's getting from the art department this year? A stipend, as in cash, above expenses. She's getting *paid* to come to school here."

"It was those photos of her feet," you say. "I can still hear Paul at the English majors' party last spring: 'Christ-like, Kim, Christ-like.'

"That's why she's such hot shit in my department. It's not the quality of her work, just the fact that she strokes Paul's ego so much.

"What was it she said in workshop the other day?

'I'm trying to be more self-referential.' Right now she's interested in pieces that make allusions to her larger body of work."

I say, "But she does have a larger body of work, huh? She's got portfolios of portfolios."

You say, "Clitoridectomy. That must be what it feels like to be Kim."

The leather strap of sleigh bells on the front door slaps and jangles as the man with the hook walks into the restaurant.

He stands for a minute by the paperback and postcard racks, then walks over to talk to some friends in a booth against the far wall.

His friends take turns shaking his hand.

You smile at him, but he doesn't notice. "The man with the hook," you say.

"The man with the hook," I say.

I'm staring down at the still life on my placemat, the gritty photo of nachos, bacon and eggs, chicken in white cream sauce.

I move my mug to the side, lift the sheet of paper up off the table, the tiny mechanical Benday dots, the blurred overlap of primary colors.

Three dishes on a checkered tablecloth. "Good Food" curving across the top in a cursive, needle-stitched script.

There is a simulated sheen to the eggs, a border of blue hearts running the rim of the chicken dish, patches of color to indicate warmth, texture, flavor.

You look down at your placemat, too, the glyphs representing cheeseburger, chicken pot pie, potato skins thick with cheese, bacon, sour cream.

"Have you ever had the potato skins?" I say. "They look good."

You say, "They don't serve potato skins here, kiddo.

They buy these place mats through some company."

The man with the hook walks over to our booth. He says, "Mr. Wheeler. Miss...?"

"Courtney," you say. "Just Courtney."

We take turns shaking his hand.

"Just Courtney," he says. "So what's the good word?"

"Oh, I don't know . . . Saginaw? Nasturtiums?"

He smiles, taps your chin with the smooth back curve of his hook.

"You run into any more trouble with that car of yours?"

"Some trouble," you say, "But no more flames."

He's already walking away. He catches the younger waitress by the pie case, slaps her ass with his good hand. The waitress leans up on her toes, kisses him on the cheek.

You look down at the flecks of black polish on your fingernails.

You sigh.

"So," I say. "Sloan. Tomorrow."

You shake another cigarette out of your pack, tap it filter down on the tabletop. You flick a bit of loose tobacco from the lip of paper at the end.

You squint across the restaurant, cradling the unlit cigarette in your palm. You bite your cheek, and you shrug.

"The other thing, kiddo. I mean, he's *always* saying things like that. Sure, he's never come down to visit, but he has called and *told* me he was going to come down to visit. It's just—I know this, but I let myself get worked up, maybe even excited. As if things aren't what they are.

"But then he'll call either really late tonight or really early tomorrow morning. He'll have a perfectly good excuse for not being able to make it down, and he'll be sad about it.

"He'll say, 'Babe, babe, I'm sorry, but…' That's sort of a code, I think. That's how Sloan starts all of his substantive statements to me.

"'Babe, babe, I'm sorry, but I just can't wear those things.

"'Babe, babe, I'm sorry, but I can't pay my part of it just yet.'

"The boy is like one of those sweepstakes mailings. He doesn't mean to come across as such an asshole so much of the time. It's just, you know, the worst thing: The way I *love* him."

You lift the candle to your face. Fire, you inhale.

There is the subtle pop as your lips release, and smoke, a bit of two-tone hair across your forehead, dishwater and bleach.

You brush it back behind your ear with a flash of guitar strings and black nail polish.

You lean down and take a drink of coffee, the flickering glow of the candle casting shadows across your face, bringing out the lines. You look much older now, harder, more like yourself.

I say, "I don't even think about Padhya anymore. I just don't even think about her, not at all."

You smile, slightly, through your cigarette.

You say, "A couple weeks ago, I sent Sloan some poems. Some about him, some about other things. And he didn't say anything, you know, not till I asked him. One day I said, 'Hey. So did you get those poems I sent you?' I mean, he's never *read* anything, either. He's just not—But I thought, you know, one time. So I asked him, and the only thing he had to say, the only thing he had to say was, 'Well, babe, things didn't happen like that. We weren't in the car when we had that talk.'

"He said, 'But it was summer.' He said, 'You know I'm allergic to fish.

"'We were coming from the pool. There was no ice on the street.

"'I don't remember the radio, but there's no cemetery on Wyandot.

"'And why do you keep saying hospital instead of clinic?

"'And what's God got to do with it? Neither of us is religious, right?'

"And he said, 'But I guess scrape is a good word. And I like how you talk about being numb.

"'But you kind of make me sound like an asshole, babe.

"'I mean, I didn't force you into anything.'"

Autumn presses against us.

You are crying, frowning down at the stub end of cigarette extending from the ashtray.

You open your mouth to speak, and you start to cough. You crumple over, a hand over your mouth, a hand holding back your hair.

You can't even smoke. He's taking everything away from you.

* * *

Autumn, to stumble and succumb, season of stain, this locked cycle of desiccation, exquisite decay, a red window, the engines of sixteen-wheelers roaring in idle behind the blinds.

The inevitability of autumn, the way the edges of flapjacks brown in sputtering grease, the nature of decomposition, leaves like cold, wet fire lending putridity to dusk.

And shifting strands of suede fringe, the yellowed creases of your jacket as you lower your head, let it rest, heavy, in your hands.

Autumn, and you cry, crouched over the red glass globe of the candle, red vinyl creaking as you lean back against the booth.

You wipe your eyes, once. Something shimmers in the fabric of your shirt, an orange spark, and you pick up your cigarette again. You take a long, hard drag and return to yourself, unfazed.

"Kim was saying this is all karmic. Kim says maybe in a past life Sloan and I had some conflict or something. She thinks we have some important issues to resolve. From, like, *Atlantis*."

"And what did Kim do in her past life? How'd she end up like she is?"

"I think it was Catholic school, kiddo. That's what her poems seem to say."

"In painting she's big on spirals, circles. Her womb, she says, is a circle."

"Ugh. Her ass is a circle."

You finish your cigarette, trace another rote constellation across the base of the ashtray.

The waitress stops at our booth with the coffee pot.

You cover your cup with your hand. "And no more for him, either," you say. "He gets so excited."

The waitress is silent, leaves us with the bill, facedown.

Autumn. You kick my shin under the table.

"'We weren't in the car when we had that talk.'"

"Alright," I say. "Let's get out of here."

* * *

On the wall behind the cash register there's a picture of a barn-raising, a rocket plane over Fort Defiance, the head of someone I think is supposed to be Zane Grey.

You steal a peppermint from the padlocked box with

its coin slot, its sticker about birth defects. You drop some nickels into the can with the photo taped to its side, a local boy born with AIDS.

I wait for change, staring down at the pie case, the old pies, corollas of baked clay, crusty glazes of sugar, fruit straining against slashes in their flesh.

And the light hangs like gauze in the alcove between the doors, that little glass room between one place and the next, the restaurant and the world, the thickness of glass, everything red, luminescent, on fire with light, the stack of free classifieds, the messages tacked to bulletin boards, babysitters needed, quilts for sale, and sorghum, and flyers for the County Fair.

You push the door open against the wind, squinting off at that heavy flow of sun, that dying pulse, the falling horizon.

* * *

We follow night down from the hills, a thousand stars winking in their sockets up above us as we pull off at the gravel drive of the yard art store.

Electric lamps hum like locusts over the lot, and the geese cast long shadows, geese like gravestones, parallel rows of cold gray concrete, geese and pineapples, planting baskets, bird baths, giant toads, midget jockeys, lions, eagles, self-contained waterfall units, fat gray sows.

Kim reloads her camera as she walks toward us, tripping every few steps, nearly dropping the camera over a low, flat-top concrete mushroom surrounded by a picnic party of concrete fairies.

"Happy to see you?" she says. "I knew you two would be late, but an hour and twelve minutes? Really, I think that's a little bit beyond inconsiderate, guys. I hate to be extreme, but I could have been *gang raped* out here.

Hello, lonely girl, remote, deserted location? Don't you two ever watch the *news*?"

You drew up your reply before we left the restaurant: "Just think of it as an experiment in sculptural uses of time," you say.

Kim pouts down at her camera bag, slips the canister of used film into a side pocket, pulls out a stack of notebooks, shuffling around for the one she wants.

She opens the notebook and begins to write as a wind picks up, sharp with chill, scuttling clumps of leaves around the saints and the virgins, the gazebo full of gnomes.

"I'm surprised it's deserted," I say. "I always imagine this place as swarming with people."

"They *were* busy," says Kim. "When they were *open*."

She lifts up her camera, looking at me through her viewfinder as she adjusts the focus. The lights catch the glitter of the plastic patch cereal ad on her t-shirt, the slick skin of her pink ski jacket.

"Big sale on squirrels today. Squirrels were half off. You should have come earlier and bought a squirrel. They have plastic or concrete, with these screws for you to fix them to a tree trunk. There was a crowd for squirrels, but the store closed at four o'clock, and I've been pretty much waiting to get raped and dismembered ever since."

"You should really ask Bear for some tranquilizers," you say.

"I don't *need* drugs, Courtney. I have art. And I am so glad I made you drop me off here this morning. It's like a big brainstorm, this place, like tarot cards, like television. Fantastic.

"I got such great pictures. Great pictures just take themselves in a place like this. Did you guys notice the leaves today? They were, like, *really* changing, absolutely brilliant colors, contrast. I can't wait to see how it all comes out in black and white.

"Luckily I brought lots of films so I could really experiment, test new ideas. I'm playing with exposure now. You guys stand there, then when I raise my hand, just turn and slowly walk away, ok?"

"Lighter," you say.

She fishes a silver lighter out of her pocket, hands it to you. Then she lifts up her camera, aims at us, fires off the flash.

We turn and slowly walk away, a series of flashes behind us.

"The surrealism of the banal," says Kim, scribbling something in one of her books.

The store itself is to our left now, a thin strip of a building, long and low, without windows. Country Fantasies markets nostalgia and its collectibility: Not only is there the yard art and the yard art clothes and accessories, they also sell shot glasses for every state, souvenir spoons, Christmas ornaments, Amish oak microwave and TV stands, barrels of stamps, geodes and polished stones, potpourri, handmade candy sticks, butterscotch...

Kim smacks her tongue against the roof of her mouth. She says, "I really need some gum, like, badly. Either of you guys have any gum?"

You cup your hands and light your cigarette, propping your boot on the swollen spherical breasts of a concrete mermaid.

Your cigarette gets going, and you tip the mermaid over. She falls face down, her nose suspended several inches from the ground by the shelf of her breasts.

Kim says, "How about it, Martin? Any gum? Just a piece?"

She makes a face, then notices the fallen mermaid.

She kneels down by it, fires off a few more shots with flash.

"Such contradiction. Rich visual irony. Have you decided on a project for 3-D Design yet, Martin? You could get some ideas here. I have plenty of notes if you want to look them over later."

"Maybe," I say, "But I'm not in 3-D Design. You and I have Theory of Art together. The guy in 3-D design is Eddie, my roommate."

"Oh, right, sorry. I don't know why I always get you two confused. He's the one with the long hair and the goatee."

"Eddie's the one with the fear of fire," you say. "Martin has a more generalized, festering, unexplored, internal angst."

"*Dissatisfaction*," I say. "Let's use as few words as possible."

"What I want to do," says Kim, "My *concept*, right, is to take all these pictures and, like, work them in with some poems I'm writing, kind of a modern Canterbury Tales, the statues telling stories all about their past lives, their own perspectives on—"

The wind again, hard enough for Kim to shut up and turn her back to it. I shiver, pull the hood of my jacket up over my head. You just squint into it, and into the woods at the lot's edge.

"We have to get some vitamins tonight, kiddo. Strep is coming."

I wrap my hand around my neck, the cellular memory of that raw ache, the throb of dry pain.

The wind fades down, but the lamps drone on, the darkness around them. Kim is on her knees, again, looking up now, taking pictures of the lamp posts.

"Come on, Kim," you say, "Shoot's over. Time to get back to campus. You might be late for something."

"It just hurts me to leave," she says. "You should come out here, Courtney. If you're *really* interested in poetry. Writing the forms of objects. No ideas but—"

She's scribbling again, struggling to balance the mottled marble-cover composition book in her palm and keep her camera bag from sliding further off her shoulder.

You pick a fallen leaf off the crown of a concrete pineapple, star-shaped, yellow. You hold it by the stem and spin it around between your fingers.

You lift Kim's lighter, set the leaf on fire. A quick ignition, a solid tongue of flame, then the leaf lets out a line of smoke as it goes dead.

You smile, hold out the lighter. You say, "Give me your hand, kiddo."

* * *

Darkness kills the scenery. Nothing remains but this ash-white road, stuttering and grainy, playing out like an aged film in the headlights. The car dips and bends, hangs for close moments, suspended in the dark. Shadows of trees press in on all sides, phantom branches scraping against glass and then gone.

Night driving, the personal significance, the hidden sense conveyed. Images flash by in fragments, like evidence. The world becomes a crime scene: The urgent curl of a mangled guard rail, the waxy reflection from a plastic floral cross, the mute horror of an isolated farmhouse.

We are listening to the hiss of radio static, constructing patterns from the rare burps of language and recognizable noise. Signals break apart in the hills.

Kim says, "Try W-LUV, out of Columbus. They always come in, even out here."

"We're not looking for a station," you say. "We have a station."

"He told me he's playing a theme tonight," I say. "Carts for lost causes."

"That's us," you say.

"...traps and poison..." says the radio.

"It's coming in clearer already," I say. "That's so weird, how reception always clears up after the asylum."

"Tegan says it's an energy drain," you say. "Every time they do a shock treatment they suck so much power from the main grid it cuts the broadcast strength. She had that internship there last spring, right, says every hour or so the lights would flicker and dim, the halls would fill with the stench of singeing hair."

"That's not true," says Kim. "And you shouldn't call it an asylum. Asylums are for tuberculosis."

"Ah," you say, "Tuberculosis, meningitis, rubella, mumps."

At the spiked iron gate of the women's mental facility, the static turns to rodent chirping as the college channel comes through the speakers.

"...soon suffer the same plight as the wolverine, the mountain lion, and the wolf."

You adjust the treble dial. "Prairie dogs," you say. "Eddie thinks this is a lost cause?"

"And extinction," says the radio, "Is forever."

Violins join the chirping for a heart-rending crescendo.

"He's getting more cynical," I say. "His cyst is getting bigger."

"Why don't you play Sloan's new demo?" says Kim. She's taking pictures of her hands against the back of your seat. "What's his new band called?"

"Shut Up and Suck," you say. "Have you heard the public service announcement about killer bees yet, kiddo? Tegan played it on her show last night."

"Are there killer bees in Ohio?" I say.

"Down around Cincinnati, sure. This cart, though, the cart is *in favor* of them. It turns out killer bees play a crucial role in the delicate balance of the ecosystem."

"Wait," says Kim. "Were you talking to me, or is that the name of the band?"

"Hey, song's over," I say.

Eddie Yoder speaks: "Alright, that was 'Save the Prairie Dog,' from the Western Wildlife Federation. Before that we had 'Keep Flag Burning Legal,' from the Commission on Constitutional Rights, 'Church Means Family' from those latter-day spin-doctors out in Utah, and I started the set out with a real plum of vintage propaganda, 'Words Hurt,' Council on Education and Youth, 1978. You are being indoctrinated by The Ideology of Subversion, the only place on the airwaves where you can get a full hour of public service announcements every week. The kitsch of the past is the discourse of the future."

"Oh, Eddie," you say, "That's a good one."

"Our hour together is coming to a close, but up next is DJ Bizaro with my second-favorite radio show, Retro Reverso, the only place on the airwaves where you get a full hour of your favorite eighties' dance hits played backwards. And speaking of the 1980s, I'm going to leave you with one from 1984, by repeated request from all you stoners at Hardy House. Time to get crazy with the model glue, kids. Here's the Public Health Coalition's mind-control masterpiece, 'Household Products Kill.'"

You scream and turn the radio up the rest of the way. I pound my knees with my palms. You beat on the ceiling. The crazy gaga guitar riffs start up, the sounds of cabinets slamming shut for percussion.

You sing along before it even starts:

*Your friends will die in their rooms
getting high, inhaling fumes.
If they offer bleach or spray,
tell them this: Keep those products away—*

Keep 'em in the cabinet, I sing.

*Drain cleaner may get you a buzz
but your nerves will burn out because
synapses fizzle into holes
when you snort things made for toilet bowls.*

The song's so loud that we can't hear the bells, if the bells are even ringing. The gate isn't down, but you slow for the red warning lights of the track anyway, just as the train rockets out of nowhere, a blast of light.

Your head presses against my shoulder as you spin the wheel, the car shifting to the right with a sound like the blades of scissors closing, and I slam against the door, a flat metal wall of train roaring past.

My mouth is full of cotton, everything drowned in sound and metal, then slats of light, quickening. The train breaks down into individual cars, rumbling at a steady pulse.

I'm staring up as the word "HYDRA-CUSHION" streaks by in letters longer than my legs.

"Fuck," says Kim.

But she has a way with that word so that it sounds like someone stepping on a prairie dog.

"Fuck," she says.

She's on the floor behind my seat.

I rub my arm, staring at the train as it passes inches from your window, as it passes without parts of our bodies hanging from it, just the crest of the Union Pacific, that evil kitty of CSX.

"Courtney," I say. "Are you ok?"

You press your palms hard against the horn, let out a whoop. You lean forward, stretching your arms out behind you.

"Am I bleeding?" says Kim. "Is this blood? We almost fucking *died* just then, Courtney. I mean, seriously, guys. I am going to have to stop riding with you. *Negligence* is not too strong a word here." She's climbing up between the seats, straining toward the rear-view mirror.

You pull the mirror off and hand it to her. "You're young, Kim," you say. "You can put it in a poem."

"What happened to the radio?" I say.

"It just kicks off sometimes." You beat your fist against the dashboard. "There."

The frequency returns, smeary, foreign sounds, a hiss in the background.

"Hey, the Satan show," you say.

You try to turn up the volume, but it's at max. You twist the bass dial instead.

We sit here parallel to the railroad tracks with the train shuttling by, the car shaking, barely able to make out the backward beat.

Kim checks her camera, detaching various parts, firing off a flash. Flatbeds rattle past, strapped with spools of metal, a pair of Case mini-dozers.

"I think it's that German girl," you say. You are yelling. "The one about bombs."

"Balloons," I say. "I know that song."

"It sounds better this way," you say.

Kim says, "Just thank *whatever* my camera didn't break. Like, you would have had to pay for that. And this is a new lens, and I have all my filters in—"

With a series of empty flatbeds, the train trails off headlong into the night. There is a silence, which is filled with sound, just less sound than before.

You gun the engine, the car jumping backwards. We spin around in a cloud of dust, jerk to another stop as you kick into forward.

You look both ways and honk before you roll over the tracks.

The receding lights of the freight train are swallowed by darkness. The music, familiar but without any clear association, like set pieces from dreams, burbles in an underwater voice.

DJ Bizaro does a voice-over to the song, speaking in the same weird slur as the vocals: "Kill your goldfish. Kill your mother. Satan is sweet as cotton candy."

* * *

Dissatisfaction?

I remember one summer night with Padhya's family at their favorite family steak house, just down the highway from the Button Museum, her father asking me yet again what I plan to do to support myself, her mother answering for me, or apologizing, at least, saying, "They're young, dear. He'll change his mind."

As Padhya sawed her steak into small cubes, cutting along a grid, raking the pieces to the side, along her untouched baked potato, eating, in the end, nothing.

* * *

Two two-lane highways cross in the middle of Northern Ohio, old Indian trails made straight, intersecting in a town half hills and half swampland, and that only half drained, a land of rich limestone soil, the legacy of glaciers. There is a factory manufacturing industrial scrub brushes, and there are those things native to this part of the state: The tire trade, chemical plants, Amish settlements, and a college, the last founded by abolitionists as a hub on the underground railroad, a place to learn Latin and Greek while helping fugitive slaves smuggle themselves into Canada.

A scenic little college, it just made the cover of the AAA Ohio travel guide. Ours prides itself on remaining a very pretty, and very correct, academic institution. We have one of the nation's premier campus composting programs, one of the nation's finest college art collections. We have very few successful suicides. Hard drug use is kept quiet. Gay-bashing and racist incidents are rare, except around exam time. The Judicial Council annually votes new penalties for rape, including expulsion. Students at our peer colleges, we are told, annually vote our school the one within the geographic region they'd most rather be attending.

Our peer colleges, nestled on their own hilltops, manicured lacrosse fields overlooking their own steel mill and tire factory towns, towns heavy with the failures of the past, a steady decline starting sometime before the Civil War, farmers farming less, industries moving away.

Slag heaps in weedy, overgrown rail yards, the brick husks of abandoned buildings, faded ghost signs on their walls.

The tune tapers out as we turn into the town proper: Streets of blank-faced houses, grim churches selling prophecy.

Kim says, "Did you hear? Some townies attacked a first-year in the parking lot of Zeisberger's Market. They beat him unconscious with his own skateboard."

"Somebody we know?" I say.

"No. I forget his name. He's from California. The campus paper ran a story, had a picture of him. You haven't read it yet, I guess. He's kind of a cutie, but he's in a concussion."

"You're never *in* a concussion," you say. "You *have* a concussion. Pain is something that you bear."

Coils of razor wire along the fence of a lot full of semi trailers. A windowless, vinyl-sided daycare warehouse. A Victorian manse, windows boarded, porch sealed off with police tape.

The next song is sped up, a frenzy of twittering vocals and the trill of what used to be a guitar.

"New song," I say. "I don't know . . . I think maybe that one from *The Breakfast Club*? No, no, Pretenders, 'Night in My Veins.'"

"Could be," you say. "I'm going with the 'Land Down Under,' but I don't know who sings it."

"Men at Work. Kim? Guess the song?"

"Think eighties, Kim. Remember? Braces and a perm?"

Kim groans.

"Dream Academy, 'Life in a Northern Town,' but it's a creepy show, not to mention stupid."

* * *

Tuesday night where two highways meet, a three-lane circle around the town square.

The fountain, dead, just a concrete trough humped with black garbage bags hauled here and dumped, leaves batting around in the wind, the clock tower looming on the court house, cars like carrion birds, hours of six-pack-draining circles, empties lobbed at the fountain or anything with an out-of-state plate, the facades of these buildings identical to the painted wooden silhouettes for sale at Country Fantasies, a tribute to the thousand small towns of the interior, quilt cozy, sharp at the edges.

DJ Bizaro starts his voice-over again. "Hide the knives. Hide the cutlery."

You shut off the radio and narrow your eyes on the lines of the road, merge into the middle lane.

The pickup in front of us swerves over by the outside curb, the passenger spitting a neat arc of tobacco juice against the window of the drug store's ice cream counter.

There's a baseball bat in the rifle rack, a Biblical citation on the bumper.

"Hoodlums is an appropriate term," says Kim. "Thugs. Felons."

From the steps of the bank, a couple of sock-capped little kids toss bits of gravel into the traffic. A stone pings off the hood of your car.

The women in the car behind lean on the horn and shout obscenities out their windows at the kids. They toss a forty-ounce bottle, which shatters on the sidewalk under the red and green awning of the Chinese and American restaurant.

"I resent the fear that I experience in this circle at night," says Kim. "I'm *sure* the people who trashed my car are here *right now,* like probably driving around behind us, spray-paint cans under their seats."

"So your parents will know to buy American next time, Kim," you say. "And think about the pictures you took."

I say, "Christ-like, those pictures of your smashed-up car."

* * *

The scorched porch pillars of Overflow One stand as sentinels on either side of the concrete steps, soot-black streaks running up the walls behind them.

Last winter, when the land's famine tightened to its hardest knot, a season of frozen hunger, the squirrels began to gnaw through anything, eating rubber-sided trash cans, newspapers, a gutter off the Alumni Center, and the rubber insulation around the electrical wiring of the house where I live.

Eddie and I walked home from the cafeteria that week before finals wondering about the smell of smoke till we came to our house and watched as the windows of our room blew out in quick splashes of glass, inky plumes spewing from the gaps.

We stood in the street and watched the blaze, the firemen making jokes about chestnuts, Wollinski rushing past them, back into the burning building, to save a sentimental four-foot bong.

And that night we all got stoned, the firemen telling stories of fires hibernating in recliners, smoldering for weeks, the size of a cigarette butt, only to explode and consume whole city blocks.

That started Eddie's terror, the speed and force and finality of flame...

Kim steps out of the car to take my seat, clicking off a few shots of the ruined awning, our boarded-up attic window, the bare bulb above the new front door.

"Ah," I say. "The burned-out homestead."

Kim says something in favor of the scene, spouting out some sort of French phrase. You roll down your window, blow me a kiss as I head for the house.

"Don't take too long checking those messages," you say. "It's dark out. We should be drunk already."

"Yeah, yeah," I say. "We'll catch up on the time."

I hold up my fist as you drive away, then give a tug to the knotted cord of clothes line looped through the hole where the doorknob ought to be.

Someone's moved the fire extinguisher again, and

I bang my foot against it as I step inside, knock the canister over, send it rolling against Wollinski's door.

The hall light still hasn't been rewired, so once I close the door behind me, there's only the curdled, curtain-filtered porch light coming from the lounge. The pair of charred couches, the slouching, water-logged easy chair. The coffee table that lost its legs, now flat on the floor. Stains still coat the wall, a lingering scent. The second-floor window lights the stairwell, casting fang-shaped shadows from the broken bars, making the split in the banister's wooden sphere more gaping.

* * *

Eddie sits at his desk in our attic room, his nose nearly pressing against the magnifying lens as he works with his tweezers.

A cold draft blows through the plywood patches over both windows, and I zip up my jacket as soon as I step through the door.

"Wheeler," he says. "What's up? Just give me one sec, huh?"

He takes the cigarette from the corner of his mouth and ashes on the floor, then swings the lens back on its metal arm, wedges his jeweler's monocle in his eye and examines his work.

"You eaten yet, man?"

"Yeah. Just got back from the Amish Kitchen."

"Did you hear what they were serving at the cafeteria? Pot roast, hashed tripe, something like that. I think the vegetarian entrée was corned beef."

I look over at the dresser, where the red eye of the answering machine is blinking away.

"*Four* messages?"

"Two of them are hang ups. Although one of those has

some breathing before the actual hang up, so I'm not sure how to count that."

"Were you here for them?" I say.

"I was here for all but the breathing one, and, frankly, she's beginning to sound like the plot summary for one of those horror movies that's gone into its ninth or tenth sequel. I mean, like, how *dare* you not be here when she calls? Give me a break. And I think she's starting to suspect something, which is in itself pretty incredible, since as of today we haven't answered the phone for two complete weeks."

"I answered it that one day," I say. "Sunday."

"Oh, right. I forgot. You did pick it up on Sunday. Hell, that should have faked her out." Eddie sighs, cocks his cigarette up with his teeth. "Alright, just got to fit this one piece..."

He leans closer, rolling a plastic rod in a dab of model glue, then fitting it into an intricate larger tangle.

There's a tiny plastic Yield sign, a pair of overturned balsa-wood picnic tables, a square of pop can aluminum ridges to look like a sheet of corrugated roof.

"The barricade?" I say.

He nods.

"I saw the burial of the Constitution at the Art Center after class. It looks great."

He nods again. I watch as he fits a couple of miniature tires against the outer wall of the student barricade, then I go over to my bed and sit down.

Our room is as long as the house, but slanted, the ceiling built along the tilt of the roof, leaving only a slim corridor down the middle where it's high enough for us to stand.

There were windows at either end, though they blew out in the fire and still haven't been replaced. They are currently boarded over, poorly, with planks of wood.

Our walls and ceiling are covered with pictures of Kent State. Photos of the events, of various campus buildings before and after, maps, those diagrams from the investigation, then Eddie's own charts, measurements, scale comparisons, one-dimensional studies, plans and patterns and blueprints for what will undoubtedly be the definitive diorama of the May Fourth Massacre: The archery shed. The pagoda. The Victory Bell.

There's a half-melted hunk of yellow plastic nailed to the sloping ceiling above Eddie's bed, the remains of the regional 4-H trophy he won senior year of high school for his Dealey Plaza.

Ten feet long, this piece, radio-controlled, the convertible taking the corner and coming down the road, a little Ken-doll Kennedy with a spring-loaded section of skull.

Dealey Plaza is still on a tour through the high schools of the Midwest, and, as such, was one of the few things that didn't get ruined in the fire.

In response, Eddie keeps everything he can in luggage or boxes, a duffel bag under his bed, an old wooden suitcase under the desk, other pieces stowed in various houses around campus, his clothes, notebooks, important sketches and designs. He has some fear that the fire might come back.

"Alright," he says, spinning around on his stool. "Done for tonight." He claps his hands together, and they stick, slightly. "The tip punctured wrong earlier," he says, working his hands apart. "Too much glue."

I take one of his rags, wipe at his hands, the palms red and pulpy, his fingers scored with razor nicks, a piece of balsa wood stuck to his pinkie.

"That's a subjective matter, Eddie, *too much glue.*" I lift the rag up, hold it over my nose.

He snubs out his cigarette, then cups his hands in

front of his face. "Hair of the dog," he says. "So have you heard the latest on Tegan? Sleeping Ugly? Or the scandal at the station?"

"Uh-oh. She fucked up with the hair dye again?"

"Last night, Tegan played this new cart, right, this PSA about date rape called, uh, 'Does This Sound Like Pleasure?'"

"This wasn't the killer bee one?"

"This was the date rape one, with the sound of some girl getting raped and this narrator saying, 'Does this sound like pleasure?'"

Eddie's pulling a sheet of skin off the side of his left hand.

"Arousing in that disturbing way that inspires self-loathing and dispersed sexualized guilt," he says. "Tegan made a bootleg of it; I can play it for you later. Anyway, she hadn't heard it before, but she played it, and then one of the members of the board of trustees called the head of the studio to complain, saying that it was too explicit, too violent, whatever. And I guess Tegan said something on the air about how it was, you know, titillating, or however Tegan would say something like that."

"Tegan wouldn't say *titillating*."

"Ok, so she said something about *moist*. I don't remember all the details, or, if I do, the details make me feel naughty. It was funny at the time. She's a damn good DJ."

"The trustees listen to the campus radio station?"

"One of them listens to her show, at least. It's because she plays *music* in between the commercials, man. It's not like I haven't tried to talk her out of it. Music is such a passing fad in radio."

"So she's in some kind of trouble now?"

"We all are, I guess. The station's going to 'reassess

the relevance of our public service announcement collection.' A purging of the archives."

"No more household products?"

"I dubbed about fifty of the best ones during my show tonight," he says. "But that's only half of her troubles, or, like, fifteen percent of her troubles. There's also this crisis with *Bear*."

"She finally saw him naked? How had she managed to avoid it for so long?"

"This is serious," he says. "Our friend Bear found himself a new favorite drug, ordered it from one of his safari supply catalogues. Yesterday this crate shows up at Hardy House, and inside, an air rifle, tranquilizer darts, a full kit for hunting and tagging some kind of large marine mammal. I think it was walruses, but I get all those creatures confused. One of the big ones, bigger than a muskrat, bigger than an otter."

"Bigger than Bear?"

"Much bigger. The dosage was for something, like, Shamu size."

I lie down on my bed, spread out my arms, stare up at the flashing green lights, the string of them stapled to the ceiling in the outline of the section replaced after the fire, a pastel I did of the Victory Bell tacked in the center.

Eddie says, "So his breathing's gone a bit *spotty*. He shot himself during Tegan's show last night, and he's been sleeping solid since then."

I sit up. My head's going fuzzy with the glue, the opposite of adhesive, a Teflon-coated brain, everything sliding away, non-stick.

"He's been *sleeping* since last night?"

"He wet himself once," says Eddie. "But he hasn't woken up at all."

"Did she call a doctor?" I say.

"There's a need to remain low profile, man. I'm

actually heading over to Hardy House now, try and see what I can do, run a little damage control."

"He shot himself? With an air rifle?"

"Yeah. Looks like. In his foot, I think. I mean, it's all very convenient, the kid can't stand needles."

"That guy is such an asshole."

"Yeah, look, I agree, but it would still be a bad thing if he died *on campus*. And Tegan's in a pretty bad place over it. She called me at the station tonight. Frazzled."

"Speaking of relationships that should not be," I say. I pull myself up from the bed, over to the dresser. I swipe at the answering machine, and the tape hisses into rewind.

A click of gears, and Padhya's voice, tinny, filtered through this black box: "Hi, Martin. I was hoping I'd catch you before dinner, but, whatever, I was only calling to say hello, and to, you know, *talk*. Last night you seemed kind of distracted, and I guess that made me start a new round of worrying about things. But, I know, I know, it's probably nothing. You and Eddie must be out somewhere, probably having a much better time than I am. At least Allie isn't here right now, and she took her rabbit with her. So, I really don't feel that bad right now, but I guess you were out somewhere when I tried to call you back last night, too. You stay out awfully late. Anyway, I don't know, how are you? This is silly, just talking to your machine. Sometimes I don't know what to think anymore, Martin. I love you. Call me."

A quick, high-pitched screech. The machine plays the first hang up, a click, the dial tone's drone, the next screech, a minute or so of distant breathing, the next hang up, then the fourth call, Padhya's sigh, breath blown and rasping against the mouthpiece.

"Me again, Martin. I guess you two are still out. You're really *never* home. Don't you all ever do *homework* or anything? Well, whatever. If you find a minute, give me a call. Check your e-mail, I've sent you a few. I forwarded this really funny thing from my mom. I sent Eddie a copy, too, if he ever uses the computer. Are you there, Eddie? Eddie, wake up. Can you hear me?"

Her fingernails tap against her desktop, the wind of Cleveland rattling her window glass. *"Alright."* Another sigh. *"Bye, then.* Love you."

I slide the volume bar down before the final screech.

"Fuck," I say. "Fuck, fuck, fuck."

* * *

Eddie is standing beside me. He puts his hand on my shoulder, makes a quick pained sound. He pulls his hand away, the glue tugging at my jacket. "Sorry," he says. "Just trying to comfort. I've got some stain remover… somewhere." He dabs at my jacket with one of his rags, the rag smelling of heavy turpentine, blotched with military-tone paint.

"It's ok," I say. "Please don't try and fix it."

Eddie holds his goatee in his left hand, wrinkling his brow. There's a spot of olive drab on my shoulder. Eddie holds the rag up to his face and takes a deep breath, offers it to me. I accept.

"Is this the scene where I offer you sage advice?" he says.

"I don't think so," I say.

"Will there be a scene like that later?"

"Maybe."

"Alright. I'll start working on it, maybe get some note cards together." He takes another hit off the rag. "Is it a soliloquy if I deliver it to another person, or is it just a monologue?"

"I think it's just a monologue."

"I'd like a soliloquy at some point. I'm beginning to think introspection is a good thing."

"Humph," I say.

"Would you say Padhya's speeches into our answering machine are monologues or soliloquies? And as long as we're on the subject, let me state for the record that I take offense at that 'Eddie, wake up' line. I was *fully* awake when I listened to that call. I was even doing *homework*."

* * *

Eddie keeps his human figures lined in rows on a fire-cracked bookshelf across from his bed. He models them from wire and putty, the degree of detail varying in accordance with placement in the scene and importance to the events as a whole, foreground versus background, protagonist victims versus the forces of oppression. The students get the most attention: Eddie worked for two weeks straight on the five-inch figure of Jeff Miller tossing back a tear gas grenade. The guardsmen are taller than the students, heavy boots, broad, squared-off storm trooper shoulders, their masks scaled larger than their bodies.

Lately, Eddie's been working on a local reaction scene, a group of citizens in a Kent barbershop, enraged over the headlines. Eddie can't get over all those letters to the editor, all the townies who went public with statements like "They should have shot 'em all," or "It's the professors they should have lined up and shot."

I crouch down to eye level with a member of one of the vigilante groups that formed after the massacre, a factory worker with his hunting rifle, ready for war, the coming Black Panther invasion.

"How did things get to this point?" I say. "When

exactly did not answering the phone become a viable course of action?"

Eddie's in front of the mirror, baring his teeth. He checks his breath with his palm, then sucks a glob of toothpaste from the open tube.

He says, "You're asking me about *love*, right?"

As he swishes the paste around in his mouth, he opens the pair of miniature scissors on his Swiss Army knife, clips at a nose hair.

"I guess so," I say. "Yeah."

"Well," he says, spitting into one of his rags. "I know that everything has to be over before it ends. Love requires a clean cut, an absolute amputation. It needs to get shot and go to sleep. So to speak."

He changes his socks, smells his boots before he slips them on, sprays a couple of shots of cologne into them, then lifts his hair and sprays some on the back of his neck.

"Take Tegan and Bear, for instance," I say.

"Take Tegan and Bear, for instance," he says. "With those two, I think it's safe to say that the critical mass has finally been achieved, that after a dozen or so months of suffering through circumstance, Ms. Bradshaw now finds herself with no other option but to take proactive steps toward the disillusionment of her present relationship."

"You honestly don't think she should have left him last spring?"

"Wheeler, love means you have to burn your bridges as you leave. Tegan's talking about dumping Bear's unconscious body somewhere in the arctic coastal regions. When she said things like that last spring it meant she wasn't sober. Last spring she was always willing to forgive him in the morning, there was always room for another chance, nothing he did was so bad that they, as a couple, couldn't recover."

I'm staring at another Jeff Miller figure, this one from Eddie's favorite photo of that day, Jeff Miller on the hill, another kid lobbing back a gas grenade, Jeff Miller with both arms in the air, middle fingers high, mouth locked in impotent rage.

"Alright, man," says Eddie. "For right now, the best thing is probably to just forget about the whole mess. Keep on keeping on. And wish me luck with everything. I'm off to Hardy House, going to test my trivial knowledge of marine biology."

"I guess I'm heading over to Courtney's, actually. I'll walk with you as far as College and St. Clair."

* * *

Here is how it happens: The rustle of wind through leaves like dried chimes, air crisp with chill and definition.

In the half-lit indigo glaze of night, slick-jacketed kids practice lacrosse passes on the sloping dormitory lawn, following the weight of the rubber ball as it arcs, brisk, the snap, the catch, the spin of the netted pole. Laughter as a stick nicks its snare, misses, drops. The ball bounces, once, then rolls our way, fast across the grass. Eddie moves and has it, hefts it up into the sky. He lets it bounce, hard, off the sidewalk, then underhands it, an easy catch, a net extended and then, in an instant, full.

We talk for a minute with the players, then set off on a diagonal across the quads, the cleat-torn mud of the practice field, the lines of pathways and dorms laid out luminous in the bare, blue bulbs atop the boxes of emergency telephones.

Past the tennis court's metal mesh fences clinking in the wind, the pools of yellowed light across the car tops and pavement of the parking lot, down a slight hill to the old oak grove.

There is a fresh layer of wood chips on the foot path, the heady scent of autumn, full-bodied, rich, and sweet.

The ridged fiber of bark, like lines of age, concentric generations kept warm in rings of sap, sending out strange waves of shadows, whisper-sharp, shivering through keen boughs.

The iron bench endowed in perpetual memory of the good souls of the class of 1913, and the path coming past, out the other end of the wood, curving up toward the Art Center, or down, concrete again, to the sparse red lights of night traffic on St. Clair Avenue.

Tremulous, the sway of the high branches, aware that this is the time of turning, anticipating flight, and freeze.

First, and simply, a view of the season, this marrow of autumn, these cracked bones of stars, senses sharpened by the bite of the air.

I turn left at the street, cross over, my fist raised for Eddie, who flashes me the peace sign as he goes his way, and I walk on alone, toward you.

* * *

There is an eternal promise that students at our college, in a far-flung, plush, and shiny future, will live in state-of-the-art dorms, dorms divided into suites with carpets and hot water in the baths, maybe even microwaves and window shades, dorms named in honor of certain tire company scions, jam cannery magnates, and princes of the industrial scrub brush manufacturing world. To this end, the administration talks occasionally of being in the midst of a major alumni donation drive, and sometimes giant cardboard thermometers are erected on the wall of the spiral staircase leading up to the cafeteria, but the temperature remains as cold as the water in the showers and most of us live in the Overflow, nine private houses purchased by the school and converted into surplus student housing, miniature dorms with drafty walls and peeling paint and problems with sewer drainage and flammability.

The toilets of your house back up into the basement and once one of the feet of one of the beds on the second floor sunk through the rotten floor, knocked loose a chunk of plaster off the first floor's ceiling which came down so hard on some foreign kid that he had to get stitches.

The stairs of Overflow Three groan and creak under each step, the slightest footfall reverberating throughout the house.

Kim's in your room, up on the third floor, but she starts yelling conversation down at me before I even make it to the second landing: "That's you, right, Martin? So when are we going to get to meet this *girlfriend* of yours? I'm, like, totally *dying* to see what she's like. I hear she's real smart. And with you, huh? I just can't *imagine*. Courtney says you and she were King and Queen of the Fall Carnival back in your high school, and like I told her, that's about as cute and small town as it gets. When you get married, you should totally hire me to do the photography. Seriously. I do weddings in the summer, you know? It's all about looking *natural*, like a really good studio shot."

Your door is open, and Kim's on her hands and knees in the center of the floor, pulling colored papers from a folder, spreading them across the rug.

She's changed her clothes since the yard art store and is now in evening wear: A shaggy blue sweater, a tweed skirt, a pair of her signature nylons.

"Nice hose, Kim."

"They've got sparkles in them."

"Oh, you're right. I just thought that was some sort of skin condition."

"Be nice, Martin. Are you sulking because Sloan's coming tomorrow?"

"You kidding me? Tomorrow night, Sloan and I are going be driving around the square together. I figure we'll huff some liquid paper, hit that new indoor archery range out beyond the K-Mart."

"I think *you're* going to have to lay low while he's in town. But I'm *so* excited to meet him. I love that Weak Chin tape. I made a dub of Courtney's copy, took it home with me over the summer. I played it for some guys I know back in Detroit, like, guys in the music scene, and they all agree that Sloan has real potential."

I study the Shut Up and Suck poster tacked to the wall above your desk, a drawing of Kurt Cobain's face, his sad, floating eyes, the barrel of a shotgun pressing against his lips.

"So where is Courtney, anyway? And does she know you're in her room?"

"She's just down in the laundry room. You know, clean sheets and panties. Getting ready for the big *visit*. But I think what she really *needs* is some incense for this room, a nice Mystic Sandalwood, Spring Shower, Mellow Morning Mist… any flavor, really. Do you like incense? I'm turned on to it right now, so powerful, you know, a real spiritual resonance. Brandon got some packages of a really great kind, authentic, from Nepal. Secret monastic recipe. They make the best incense, the Nepalese. They're Buddhists. They use it to meditate."

"How *is* Brandon? Feeling better?"

"He's fine."

"Still under surveillance, is he?"

"Depression is a chronic, clinical illness, and

recognition of the condition is the first step toward a cure."

She kneels on one knee, adjusts herself, yanking at her hems, tucking hair back behind her ears, pulling her sweater down over a ripple of flesh at her back.

"So what's in the folder, Kim?" I say.

"Just some poems. Courtney wanted to see them. She's really working on her style, you know. She has some potential, too, but she still needs to find her own unique voice. She needs more experience, some discipline. She's a lot like you in that respect. I keep thinking about those pieces you submitted to the Art majors' show last spring—"

"But enough about me," I say. "Let's talk about you."

"Well, ok, I was almost published last month. This little magazine back in Detroit. Well, *journal*, I guess. Avant-garde, literature and theory, a lot of stuff about, like, politics, identity, the body. And, now, I know what you're thinking, but I didn't give head to the editors or anything like that. I happen to know this girl who used to date one of the former—one of the *founding*—editors, but that doesn't count. That's just happy coincidence. I mailed my poems in unsolicited, same as anyone else."

"Kim, you don't do *anything* the same as everyone else."

"True, true," she says, smiling.

I sit on the corner of your mattress, on the old, gray wool blanket stamped US NAVY, your guitar next to me, propped on its red velvet floor pillow with its stringy gold fringe. On the tie-dye-draped plastic milk carton next to the bed sit your alarm clock, your stack of nightmare notebooks.

Kim's still shuffling the papers around on the rag weave rug, pink sheets and purple sheets, pea green, pearl gray, plum.

She says, "It's so good something like that is happening in Detroit, you know? A real attempt at intellectual and artistic activity, the spark of a new renaissance. Detroit could be a pretty decent city if people just put in a little more *effort*."

"Are those poems?" I say.

"My poems. Just some of them, of course, not necessarily the best, but a representative sample. Want me to read?"

"Which one is getting published?"

"*Almost*," she says. "They said that although they were unable to accept my work at the time, I'm welcome to submit again in the future. And they thanked me for the opportunity to read my pieces."

* * *

As you climb from the basement, Kim and I hear every step.

Kim yells at the door when it sounds like you're halfway up: "Hey, Courtney. Martin here thinks he's going to spend tomorrow night circling around the square with your boyfriend, just driving around, seeing the *sights*. How about that? I tried to tell him that *maybe* things aren't going to be happening *exactly* like that, but Martin's stubborn about things. Pretty funny, though, those two driving around together, don't you think? Courtney?"

I hear you slow down, hear you let her wait. She kneels in her nylons, watching the door as you finish the last flight, slowly, working an extra squeak from each step.

You walk into the room and take a long, focused pull on your cigarette. The flame catches, hisses back through the paper with a dull rush as you inhale.

You drop your armload of laundry beside me on your bed, then run your hand through my hair, brush your knee against my arm.

You exhale, loading your words before you speak: "Best plan yet, kiddo. You two can have a conversation in the car. He just loves *those*."

"You're just in time, Courtney. I was about to read one of my poems for Martin. Now you can hear, too. Let me see, which one should I start with?"

"Just in time, kiddo." You dig your nails into my scalp.

"Oh, and hey, Courtney, do you have, like, a *light* someplace? I looked through your desk, but I couldn't find anything. Matches, maybe? I don't know what happened to *my* lighter, but I'm really upset about it. It was a present, from a boy, real sweet, a token of affection. It was silver, and it had my name on it, and I know I had it at that lawn decor place, but do you think I left it there? I hope maybe it's in your car somewhere. There was that *accident*, right? Maybe I dropped it."

"What are you talking about?" you say.

"My lighter. My cigarette. A light?"

She holds up a soft pack of cigarettes, some kind of floral design on the front.

"Try the stove," you say, "Downstairs."

You walk over to her arrangement of papers, pick one up, a pink one.

"'Fleshy curtains of...' Ugh. And what's with this paper?"

"The stove? Like, the pilot light or..."

"Oh, fuck it," you say. "Give me one, I'll light it off mine. Oh, Kim, what the hell kind of cigarette is this?"

"It's a new kind. Whole Tone." She scoots back, pushes your gold foil ashtray to the center of the rug. "Want one?"

Lighting her cigarette, you cough, spitting it into your palm. You try again, then light another of your own for yourself.

"Some kind of microbrew brand?" I say. "Honey-roasted, recycled tobacco?"

"Ice brewed, it tasted like."

"They're just not as *bad* for you as other cigarettes," says Kim. "Less chemical additives, something. I don't know, but they taste better."

She picks up the pack again, turns it over. The back is covered in small-print text, which she moves her finger over as she reads, searching for an appropriately convincing quote.

"Kim, they're cigarettes. They are going to kill you, and you are going to die."

"They're all made in the same factories," I say. "Oh, but the pack's kind of pretty, made of pressed leaves and flower petals. And a traditional Native American prayer printed on the back, all about ambient beauty and saving the planet for future generations."

"Alright," you say, "Everybody has to stop talking so I can read this *poem*."

You drop the pink sheet and pick up another one, dark purple.

"Kim, did it ever occur to you that these are a little hard to read?" you say.

"My printer's running out of ink."

"Here, you read this one, kiddo."

"Want *me* to read it?" says Kim.

"Martin reads better."

"But," says Kim.

"This *is* hard to read," I say. "Hand me another one, will you? One with the ink and the paper in *different* colors."

You laugh, standing by the window, your cigarette between your fingers. You pick some dry fronds from the hanging fern, drop the dead plant pieces into your palm.

I pick a piece of peach paper, clear my throat a few times. You pull over the trash basket and watch the dead pieces spin and flutter as they drift down.

I say, "This one's called 'Sexual Awakening at the Saint Anne Parish School.'"

"My fern is *sick*, kiddo. Look."

You unhook the pot from its ceiling chain and carry it over to me, drop it into my lap. The fronds are freckled with red spots, with tiny, crusty patches.

"Scale," I say. "I think that's what this is. Some kind of insect, maybe a mite."

"Sure you don't want *me* to read *my* poem?"

"A gateway infestation," you say. "First mites, then bedbugs. Vinegarroons. Land crabs."

"Bedbugs?" says Kim. "*That* could be a problem."

I put the fern on the floor, brush some potting soil off my pants, off your blanket.

You lift the pot back up, squint down at the plant, poke at a frond with the end of your cigarette.

"This just had to happen now, didn't it? Everything at once. You know how I got this fern, kiddo? I got this fern right after Mom went nuts. My *aunt* drove out to the farm and helped me load up all my stuff. She drove me straight over to Sloan's, then she went out and bought us a couple bags of groceries, you know, 'some stuff to get you two started.' Cans of concentrated lime-aid, packages of powdered donuts, some cracked-wheat crackers, some potted meat product, a family-size plastic squeeze bottle of ketchup, a Mylar balloon shaped like a dinosaur, and this stupid fucking fern, a little shiny Good Luck sign stuck in its dirt."

"There's got to be a spray," I say. "They make medicine for everything."

"We have to save this fern, kiddo. Help me, ok?"

"We'll go out to K-Mart. Plant medicine. It'll be no problem."

You stare at the fern for a few more minutes, then sigh, hang it back on its hook in front of the dark window.

Kim stands up and adjusts her bra. "Guys?" she says. "Not really in a poetry kind of mood right now?"

You say, "I'm in a mood for liquor. I'm in a mood for insecticide."

* * *

The town's main drag is four lanes wide, lined with strip mall storefronts and franchise restaurants, the North end of the North-South highway.

Here the cars don't circle, they race, gunning their engines in front of swinging stop lights before roaring off, running sometimes as far as the Interstate.

"Did you see that?" says Kim. "More swastikas."

She points to the scabby, shuttered windows of the News Stand, big spray-paint slash-whorls crossing over them.

"The high school Nazi gang. There's a big story on them in that issue of the campus paper you haven't read. A rash of vandalism. Swastikas. Sometimes stars."

"Maybe the News Stand guys just put them there for decoration," you say. "Ever been past the bead curtain, Kim? The back room?"

"Streamlined," I say. "You can rent porno and how-to hunting videos in the same place. They've got toys, too. Erotic tools."

"'The Real Life Vagina'," you say. "That's a *trademarked* phrase."

"There," says Kim. "The handicraft store."

More rough swastikas over the Half Price signs, the Cost-Cutting scissors mouthing sample spools of seasonal cloth.

"Maybe we can reconstruct this little blitzkrieg," I say. "Some kids, they buy a few cans of paint, then they go rent some bow hunting and gang bang films."

"Fly fishing and chicks with dicks," you say. "There weren't any swastikas downtown."

"They didn't hit the Steak Emporium, either," I say.

"Fascist bastards."

"All I know is what I read in the paper," says Kim. "And they didn't say *isolated vandalism*. They used the word *rash*."

The town's two major landmarks straddle opposite sides of the drag, and we pass between them. The stone obelisk in the Steak Emporium parking lot commemorates the county's last massacre, a mass execution toward the end of the Indian Wars. On the other side of the road, the ever-exploding neon pins atop the Fallin' Timbers Bowling Alley open outward like a red, white, and blue fan, searing the night.

We stop by the flashing yellow silhouette of a bottle above the entrance to Lamont's Drive-Thru Liquors, the fourth car back in the line snaking out the front.

High school kids, hands in pockets, shuffle from car to car, trying in their slouched, nonchalant way to strike up some sympathy, score a beer or two.

There's a girl to the side, scuffing her sneakers on the concrete. She looks up at you, then picks up her backpack and circles around the building.

Our turn comes, and we roll inside the converted

double-wide garage, its sides lined with shelves and refrigerated cabinets, stinking of auto exhaust and old cardboard, the selection heavy on malt liquor, beer by the forty-ounce and mini-keg, wine in boxes or with screw-tops, often carbonated, fruity.

You roll down your window, and a woman in a green apron walks over to take our order.

Kim leans up between the seats. "Do you have any Blue Jacket Stout? It's a microbrew. In little, like, *square* bottles?"

The woman looks back at the cars behind us, gives a weak nod. She has a thick ring of pink scar tissue around her neck, under her chin.

"Trivia night, Kim?" you say.

"It's *so* good, Courtney, for real. You have to try some. I know the guy who brews it. I mean, I met him once, but we hung out. He lives in Toledo. I mean, this is what he *does*. He lives in Toledo, and he makes beer."

"Alright, two six-packs of that and a carton of the Ultra Lights."

The guy who loads the beer comes to my side with the six-packs. I go to roll down the window, but the knob's gone. Kim takes the beer through her window, and the woman with the scar steps into the glass-walled booth behind the rack of skin and gun magazines to run your credit card. She comes back with the card and your cigarettes.

"Thanks, Dad," you say, slipping the card back into your pocket, stuffing the receipt into the ashtray. "Kim, why don't you give Martin one of those Little Turtle Lites?"

"It's *Blue Jacket Stout*," she says.

"Drink, kiddo. And open one for me."

"What's your father doing these days?" says Kim.

"She's French," you say. "She just lives in Canada."

"Do you ever hear from him?"

"I think he has some new kids, actually."

You drain a beer as we drive through the far end of the store.

The exit lets out into an alley, the back of a state-run residential facility for the handicapped, and you turn right, then pull to a stop next to the dumpsters.

With a rustle of fringe you wipe your mouth on your sleeve. You wedge the beer between your thighs, flash your headlights.

"Uh, Courtney?" says Kim. "Everything ok?"

The girl from the front of the store steps out of the shadows, checking the alley, the back end of the store. She walks over to your window, and you hand her the second six-pack then rip back the top of the cigarette carton, hand her a couple of packs. She passes you a wad of bills that you tighten and slip into the breast pocket of your jacket, clicking shut the shiny pearl-and-silver button.

"That beer's from Toledo," you say. "Some guy makes it."

The girl is shivering in the night, hugging the six-pack against her chest, eyes jumping from the store's exit to the mouth of the alley.

Something passes through you, too. A slight tremble. You bite your lower lip, lean down, punch in the car's cigarette lighter.

"Just thanks a lot," she says. "Usually, it's only creeps and pervs buy the beer. And they all want to trade and shit."

You say, "Yeah, well, don't share with assholes, ok?"

* * *

The empty K-Mart parking lot stretches out in cold submission under the low bulk of the night. The windows of your car steam over as we drink.

Sloan's tape is in the stereo, the Shut Up and Suck demo. You weave your hands to the rhythm, singing along with the lines you approve.

"You didn't leave me when you should have, now you leave me all the time," and *"I need what I want and that's no good."*

Sloan doesn't write the words, of course, but they still seem his to me, all I know of him that isn't from your mouth.

"They sound great," says Kim. "Easily as good as Weak Chin." She leans in between us for the car's lighter, fires up another herbal Whole Tone. She says, "Less metal, more *heart*."

I recline my seat back a few notches, prop my feet on the dashboard. The beer is cold and sharp.

You keep your eyes closed, dancing with your fingertips, your fringe, guitar string bracelets flashing as you flick your wrists.

Kim laughs, tries to cover with a quick pull on her cigarette, coughs, tries to cover it with her hand, drops her cigarette on the floor, picks it up.

"Sorry," she says. "I just keep thinking about that girl outside Lamont's. The word is *skank*. Did you see that hair? I mean, the fine line between style and nap. And she didn't even look *fifteen*, not that I'm saying you should feel bad about it. I mean, like we're any more legal. Do you *ever* get carded at that place?"

You say, "I don't get *carded*."

You wipe clear a band across the fogging windshield, the feral glare of neon and lamp light, the distant, cloud-shrouded stars, a season steady as it is bleak.

Shopping carts roll in the wind, banging against their scattered, toppled kin, abandoned earlier in the day by shoppers or the kids who come here after school to play stock cars, demolition derby.

And there is that whole ubiquitous holiness routine, the five huge, blue letters hovering above us all, an illuminating, mystic sign. And the lamps, crook-necked at intervals across the cold expanse, could almost be said to look something like monks at prayer. *Halo* being the most convenient word we have for when light rims around a bulb and in the wet window glass splits into sharp, star-like spikes, which could conceivably be compared to the adornment on certain icons, if icons were the sort of thing a person knew better than lamps in a cold parking lot at night. Sloan's somber delivery, plodding against the backs of the speakers: *"Life is a lot of things. Life is a lot of things. Life is a lot of things."* A single droplet beads up toward the top of my window, and a tear runs down the glass.

"Do you think they're better?" says Kim, "That this band will do better than Weak Chin?"

"Weak Chin opened once for a band in Cleveland," you say. "That's probably as good as it's going to get."

"I *loved* them."

"So did I. For a long time."

"It's too bad they broke up, huh?"

You tilt back and finish your second beer, concentrating on the rings of light, the streaks that shine in the glass of the windshield.

"So what are we doing tonight?" says Kim.

"Won't make any difference," you say.

* * *

And so we go inside to shop for insect poison.

Through the double set of hissing automatic doors, the alcove of spilled employment and apartment guides, quarter vending machines of super bounce balls, rubber snakes, and temporary tattoos.

The field of check-out lanes, the lone cashier spreading a newspaper over her scanner, the lane light above flashing silently for assistance, Express, Express, 12 Items or Less. "Closing in half an hour," she says. "And the floor's wet."

"Everybody goes to the 24-Hour Super Walmart these days," says Kim. "Nobody comes out here anymore. It's depressing and passé, even for the poor."

"Well, Kim," you say. "Our lives are a little clichéd."

The acne-faced kid ragging down the snack bar gives your ass a weary look, then rolls his gaze over Kim, who tilts her head to the side and smiles.

And at the counter, the finger-thin franks turn on their electric spits, plump grease pimples straining against their red skins.

There is the constant sloshing grind of the Icee machine, charred husks at the bottom of the empty popcorn popper.

"Have you noticed, kiddo? Kim's wearing a size too small. She says she wants a little extra definition."

Signs hang from the ceiling, spinning in the re-circulated breeze, their colors reflecting on the shiny black half-spheres of the closed-circuit surveillance cameras, a sale on dandruff shampoo, loose-leaf notebooks, and bow hunting equipment.

A long plastic banner stretches across the main aisle, the far-right end broken loose and draping down over a display of children's camouflage jackets. "SALE," it says, along the vertical. The part still up reads, "THE BIG FALL."

You nod, drag your thumb across your lower lip.

"That's so fucking true," you say.

* * *

"So what *is* happening tonight?" I say.

"Well, first off, Brandon will probably OD on Dimetapp or something. Right, Kim?"

"Come on," I say.

Kim says, "He was depressive last week."

"And the week before?"

"He slips through phases. It's depression. Depression is a chronic, clinical illness, and recognition of the condition is the first step toward a cure."

"That's how Padhya talks, isn't it, kiddo?"

"Come on," I say.

"Yeah, Courtney."

Kim searches around for something else to say, anything, away from us. She settles for "I wonder if they have that new CD?"

"Go look," you say. "Martin and I have to get high and check out the hunting equipment."

* * *

The tiles are sticky under our soles, aisle after aisle, a lusterless oblivion lit by receding parallels of tube lights.

The washed-out pallor of discount sweat suits, the smell stuck somewhere between damp cardboard's bland rot and bulk kitty litter's sickly, lung-tightening sweet.

Easy Listening churns around us. Owl-shaped ceramic lamps, surfaces pearly as petroleum spills. A half-eaten jar of mashed beans with bacon baby food.

You steer straight for the pharmacy, the over-the-counter cures, select a box of allergy medicine and a box of weight-loss supplements.

Your rip open the cardboard, pop pills out from their foil backing, counting them out in your palm, mixing cocktails of white-trash uppers.

"Safe as coffee," you say.

We each dry-swallow a handful. You open a box of condoms, slip the two strips into the pockets of your jacket, fold the box closed again, place it back on the shelf.

"So what's all this about Bear? Eddie said some kind of drug designed for walruses."

"California sea lion, actually. Tegan's pretty overwhelmed."

"Close enough," I say. "Eddie's notoriously bad with mammals. Sometime he still talks about how rats started the fire."

"Yeah. I've thought of some more good ones, though, since we're in this section: Rheumatism, hepatitis, spastic colon... What's the other one? Colitis."

"Poetry in nature," I say. "There's already a rhyme there. And you could just cheat a little, end the next line with psoriasis."

"Oh, that's even better. Psoriasis. Good associations. So classical sounding, like a warrior goddess, some doomed seer."

"Some doomed seer? You get dramatic when you hit the Blue Jacket brew."

"It's the setting, kiddo. Look around you: Hair tonics, lice combs, enema kits, stool softeners."

"Eye patches," I say. "Corn pads."

"Cotton balls," you say. "That can be a harsh scene, too. This place catalogues everything that can go wrong, then lists the side effects of trying to fix the problem."

"California sea lion," I say.

"I know. I told Tegan you would be sympathetic only if it was indigenous."

"Nothing's indigenous anymore. Prairie dogs are a lost cause."

"We don't even live in the prairie."

"I think that was Eddie's point. But there's prairie up near Cleveland."

"Bullshit."

"But even if it was, say, Lake Erie walleye or something, I mean, deer valium or something, the point is he's just following the natural progression of recreational use of animal medicine. All those dog pills were just gateway drugs. Then the horse tranquilizers, now these seal darts…"

"Don't forget the udder cream."

"I hadn't heard about the udder cream. But that's a whole different category. Lots of people use udder cream."

"You, kiddo?"

"I've heard it's pleasant. Good for you. Functional."

"Kiddo?"

"I've heard. Lots of people use it."

"Tegan says it's great. Bear's big, but smooth."

"Much like a sea lion, I'm sure. Why is Tegan still with that guy? All he seems to be good for is weird downers, animals medicines."

"He really loves Tegan," you say. "He makes her happy sometimes. He doesn't interfere with her being herself, and he's always around if she needs him."

"And slow enough to catch."

You're examining the cartoon instructions on the back of a boxed breast pump. An aisle of bottles and rattles, pacifiers and pregnancy tests.

"Thinking about your aunt again?"

"I wish she hadn't called."

You wedge the breast pump behind some wrist braces. Self-adhesive bandages, instant cold packs, travel cups full of pain killers.

"Pregnant was enough," you say. "But she also mentioned my mother. Then she was like, 'So, has your Sloan popped the question yet?' He's always *my* Sloan. As if other people have their own Sloans they drag around behind them."

Electronic potpourri. Cellophane bags of doll parts hanging next to Styrofoam orbs, glue guns, craft project boxes of popsicle sticks.

A life-size plastic doe hangs from the ceiling of Sporting Goods, a bull's eye centering around that place near the shoulder where she should have a heart.

"Do you two talk about marriage?"

"In high school we talked about it."

"Padhya still talks about it. Her mom talks about it. They buy bride magazines together, subscribe to some kind of e-mail list server on the astrological significance of baby names."

"Sloan brings it up when he feels really jealous or inadequate. Often."

You stand in front of the knife case, studying the serrated hook curves of skinning tools. Stainless steel teeth. Locking blades.

"So, according to my aunt, Mom's in California now. She said she got a postcard. My mother's found a religion, something to encourage her denial."

"She sent a postcard, huh?"

"Didn't mention me, I guess. I asked. I said, 'Did she mention me?' and my aunt said something lame like, '*I'm sure* she's thinking about you, honey. She *loves* you.'"

"Knee socks heated by nine-volt batteries," I say.

"Nice. The rubber overalls are quite a thing, too."

"Canned musk," I say.

You purr, rub your shoulder against mine.

"Always with the perfect fucking phrase, kiddo."

"Religion," I say.

"Read, selling flowers at a bus terminal. Or something worse. At the very least the term implies a fucked-up diet. And a *commune*. Sometimes I think all my mother's problems go back to her separation from the commune."

"Maybe she found a good one again," I say.

"Again? It wasn't a good one before, remember? As our friend Kim would say, the appropriate word here is *brothel*."

"Free love," I say. "That's something different."

"That wasn't *free love*," you say. "That was just adultery. My father was only a hippy because it was the most convenient way to get a piece of ass."

"There's the environment," I say.

"An agent falling for his own cover story. My father's only an environmentalist these days because he's getting old. He can't *handle* so much ass."

You are testing the pull on each of the compound bows, watching the way the wheels turn to distribute force, to propel death.

"Careful," I say. "You can pull an arm out of socket that way."

"No more about my parents," you say.

Shelves of hunting caps, flannel plaids and various earth tones. Camouflage patterns specific to undergrowth, season, geography, and time of day.

The texture and details of bark mimicked in fabric. The shadowy shade and overlap of foliage, moss, cobwebs, lichen, twigs… A cloak of particulars.

And all the abstract military standards. To blend

invisible, slashed in color, the green and brown of trenches, even the pre-season white and gray.

I pick a classic Day-Glo orange, a cap that radiates a feverish human warning. I try it on, tie the earflaps down under my chin.

"Did I tell you Padhya wants me to be an architect now? She said, 'You can still paint and draw and stuff, silly boy. That's what the weekends are for. Until we have kids.'

"Like everything, it was her mother's suggestion. Like the names Daniel and David for sons, Lisa and Laurel for daughters."

You hang the last bow back on its hook, run your fingers down the length of a plastic canoe as you walk past the deer slings and arrow shafts, toward me.

"It's a good look for you, kiddo."

You straighten the cap on my head, flip the brim up, then back down.

"Reversible," I say.

"Plaid on the inside. Now that's a sexy phrase. Say it for me."

"Plaid on the inside. It's not too subtle, is it?"

"Kind of a collegiate King of the Carnival thing going for it, kiddo. You can be an architect on the weekends. We can be in the car when we have that talk."

★ ★ ★

This is the state of things: An entire aisle devoted to pesticides, placed just to the lee of the slate, pine, and maroon rubber shacks of Lawn and Garden, the leaf blowers, the rakes, the decorative trash bags in "All Your Autumn Colors," the value pack quadruple sets of mouse traps, "Buy Three, Get One Free," indoor and outdoor roach motels, inflatable decoy owls and snakes for repelling noisy, migratory murders of crows.

Kim is here already, kneeling to read the labels' fine lettering, studying the silhouettes of susceptible bugs, her nylons glittery against her knees.

"There you guys are," she says, standing up, tugging down her skirt's hem. "I can't remember what those little red things are called."

"Canker sores," you say.

"Well, this one kills ants, black widow spiders, fleas, brown dog ticks, crickets, sawbugs, millipedes, and earwigs."

"Aw, Kim," I say. "Did they have your CD?"

"No, of course not. Sold out. Or kids just *stole* them all."

"No law and order," you say. "Nobody learned anything from Kent State. That's what I keep telling Eddie."

"Have you heard his latest plan?" I say. "He thinks there should be something like Mount Rushmore. Those four faces."

"Come on, you guys," says Kim. "This one's good for aphids, whiteflies, mealybugs, budworms, mites, leafminers, trips, and scales."

"Poison, poison everywhere," you say.

On the label of the spray bottle I pick up is a picture of a giant ant ripping the roof off a suburban home and its adjoining two-car garage. The label is soaked through, sloughs off in my hand.

You say, "Which do you figure has more warnings on the back: Insecticides or medicines?"

"There are an awful lot of warnings here," I say.

I shake my wrist, and the label slaps to the floor. I wipe my hand on my pants, but my palm already itches, tingles like tiny needles, begins to burn.

"So many choices," says Kim. "Isn't there someone who works here, someone to tell us what brand of poison we want?"

"Would it be an *etymologist* or an *entomologist*?"

You lift up a gallon jug of something with a scorpion on the label.

"I think just standing here is a health risk," I say.

I hold my hand up to my nose, a smell like dry powder, that deep chemical sting. I exhale, empty my lungs, hold my hand over my mouth and take another hard pull.

"Did you see?" says Kim. "They have squirrel traps, too. Maybe we should get a few of those."

"'Safe and Humane,'" you say. "Another trademarked phrase."

You pick up the display model, a folding metal cage with a trapdoor at one end and a harness hanging inside for bait, a handle at the top for transport. You turn it over in your hands, feeling its weight. You set the catch, trip it shut with your car keys, test the pull on the sprung door.

Then you set the squirrel trap on the floor in the middle of the pest control aisle.

You take a step back, one step, then you drive your boot through the side, snapping several of the thin metal rods. A broken hinge pops loose and flies across the aisle. The cage crumples.

Your second kick sends it sliding across the tile, smashing into the racks of growth formula and herbicide spray, knocking some fertilizer spikes to the floor.

You say, "Kim, do you ever think that maybe there's a world outside your consciousness?"

"I think that means we're letting the scale live. You ok, Courtney?"

"A fucking dinosaur balloon," you say. "Potted fucking meat product. And as much as I hate that fern—*always* hated that fern—I don't hate it half as much as I hate my stupid grit aunt. And, you know what, she can go to hell with herself. She's my *aunt*. She's not my fucking *mother*."

"Come on, huh? Let's just get out of here. You're inviting us up to your place, right, Kim? You've got something numbing to drink?"

"Sure," she says. "There's wine. I have to call Brandon anyway. I'm sorry, Courtney. Don't be mad at me. I didn't mean anything by anything. I was just…"

You stand with your back to us, wipe a hand across your face.

"It's ok," you say. "I just want to get away from this place."

* * *

The gurgle of the aquarium, the smell of ammonia and fresh paint.

You track black diamonds of mud across the plush beige carpet of the French Suite.

You sprinkle a few pinches of fish food into the tank as Kim puts the wine out on the coffee table. Then she runs up the spiral staircase in the corner, crosses the second-floor balcony to her room, the middle of three overlooking the lounge. She leaves her door open behind her.

Framed French posters for operas or art house films hang from the inner walls of the suite, Art Deco ivy snaking around their edges. The outer wall is one big window, three sides, arching up into a skylight ceiling, glass pressed black with night, reflecting back the room, garish against the dark, the blurred glow of my new cap, you, tilting the wine box over our mugs, twisting the plastic nozzle.

"Not so much wine left, kiddo. It'll be a short visit to Language Housing."

"No complaints," I say.

I cross over to the padded leather couch, its cushions billowy, cloud-like, the color of putty. I slump down and listen to the hiss as I sink and settle.

The giant television, tuned, as always, to SCOLA, is, as always, on mute.

Hundred-meter-long arms of farming machines turn in steady, spraying circles across the screen.

"And it's not red wine. And it's not white wine."

"How like Kim," I say. "Blush."

"Pink wine is, how you say, so *very* French, *verdad*?"

"*Si*. And *très* Kim."

We clink our mugs together.

"Here's to how the other half lives."

"Plush and shiny," I say.

"Are you listening to that, kiddo?"

"What?"

You nudge upward with your chin, cock your head to the side, toward Kim's door, where her voice rasps with the harsh desperation of a stage whisper: "Yes, it's important. Brandon. Brandon, it's *important*. No, well, just try and think. How full was the bottle this morning?"

I focus my eyes on my brim's plaid underside.

"Oh, cycles," I say. "Oh, predictability."

"She always gets louder before she starts to whisper."

"Let's just ignore her. Let's watch SCOLA and get drunk. Look, it's something exciting: Vegetables, water."

"My favorites, kiddo. But *together*? Vegetables *and* water? Some things are too dangerous to be mixed."

"Hydroponic agriculture," I say. "A documentary."

"Cheers. I'll drink to hydroponic agriculture."

"Those damn French. Look. They think of everything."

"Aqueducts. Aquifers. Those are hydroponic words."

"Endless miles of irrigation pipelines towering over the farmlands of France."

"Towering implies a vertical, kiddo. Are they really towering?"

"Come look," I say.

"Towering would be like a cock, kiddo. Even the French wouldn't irrigate like that."

"Come look, would you. Plenty of room inside the couch. I'll just scoot down a bit deeper, burrow. Here, you can have the top level."

"Water and wine," you say. "This round's on me."

You refill the mugs, perch yourself on the solid arm of the couch.

"Brandon," says Kim. "Brandon."

"That was a scream," I say.

"That was *insistent*, shot through with emotion, reflecting a certain degree of horror, true, but the scream will come after—"

"No, yes, no, I love you. How could you ever think— But, Brandon. Brandon, I love you. *I love you*."

"The scream will come after the love part."

Kim slams her door shut, then reopens it, checks the lock, slams it again.

"So much for that," I say.

"The scream will be louder than a closed door," you say.

You play with my right earflap, lifting it up by the tie, holding it out horizontal to my head, fanning me with it.

The television screen shows a pastoral landscape dotted with tanks and towers, tubes bubbling gas under giant spinach leaves.

"Channeling the living waters," you say.

"This show makes me need to piss."

"Fascinating," you say.

A French farmer holds up a basket full of softball-size

radishes, poses beside a turnip slightly larger than his head. Conveyor belts roll tomatoes, red waves.

"So waxy and plump," you say.

You refill our mugs again, spurting a little wine on the carpet. You rip the box open along its top seam, pull out the silver bladder, coax the last of the wine into my mug.

"This is it for the box, kiddo. *Adieu*, rosy blush of night."

"Does she have anything else? What else is French? Absinthe?"

"We'll go to Tegan's."

"Tegan has absinthe? I knew it. Those Hardy House stoners."

A farmer steps off his tractor to embrace some kind of squash or pumpkin.

A pair of children run hand-in-hand through a forest of carrots and celery, then board a giant aubergine and fly away to the stars.

"Absinthe and walrus tranquilizers. The new Bohemians."

Something shatters against the inside of Kim's door, and then there is the scream, a punctuation in sound—high, fast, sharp, and sudden.

"Here's to Brandon," you say.

"To Brandon," I say. "Who keeps trying."

"To old, familiar dramas. Oh, kiddo, I'm swimming."

"You're beautiful, Courtney."

"The man in the orange hat."

"I mean it."

"Sure," you say. "She's about to call security, though. Or is it the ambulance people who send security? Does she just call the ambulance people?"

Kim's sobs come through the door. Something else is thrown, something more solid, thudding against the door and falling back, heavy, shaking the walls.

"Yeah," I say. "That's definitely our cue."

"Goodnight, fish. Goodnight, France."

A copy of this week's campus newspaper is on the floor under the aquarium. I fold it in half and slip it into my jacket pocket as you sprinkle another pinch of fish food into the tank. Then you let your mug slip into the water, watching it as it sinks, the tiny bubble rising up from its edges.

The fish disperse, then circle in again, familiarizing themselves with their changed world.

Sirens sound in the distance. We leave the suite's door propped open to the hall.

* * *

I have seen the glow of headlights deep beneath the green water of Kyle's Creek, the phantom glow from the apparition of that automobile wrecked and towed out back in 1954, the star-crossed lovers and the whole rest of the tale...

Eddie and I and some other kids went out there last spring, to those swamplands west of town, though, even after witnessing the phenomenon, I remain unconvinced.

West of town is nothing but grits and white supremacists, any of whom could have rigged up a fake with some halogens and an underwater extension cord, a show for the college students who grew up on the rural legends and ghost stories of Northern Ohio.

As stories go, the Ghost Car is a pretty dumb one, not half as good as the Dead Ones of Zoar, appearing in mirrors and frosting over windows, delivering their prophetic warnings in blue-lipped High German, their old faces still frozen from that cannibal pioneer winter, their skull tops eternally scalped, steaming fresh blood.

Even Maumee's most prominent legend, the Firelands Stallion, galloping blank white with its empty saddle, running through the husky, harvested fields of late autumn to warn Mad Anthony Wayne of ambush, sounds spookier than the Ghost Car.

Defiance's luminous clergyman, standing with his lantern beside the railroad tracks to warn the next engineer of a bridge that fell back in the great New Madrid quake, Fostoria's Baby in the Bottle, forever shelved away and screaming, Sandusky's Woman of the Woods, widowed in the first World War... none of these other towns can match ours when it comes to the horror of history.

This is the town that mobbed its jail on that Christmas Day, just like in the many folk songs dedicated to the topic, irate farmers setting the building ablaze to kill escaped slave Uriah Pitt, fugitive from the Georgian plantation where both his eyes had been cut out, spending his last months wandering the North, preaching a false religion of invisible angels and coming plagues.

The jail was rebuilt in the late fifties as the local tourist commission, but in the remodeling the floor was raised two feet higher than in Uriah's day. So when his ghost is seen pacing in the corner where the cell once stood, the figure is only visible from the knees up, shuffling feet sunk in the foundation.

And this is also the town of Deborah Hardy, famed poetess, who shaved her head one autumn night during the first year of the Civil War, walked from room to room of her husband's house, pushing his shaving razor first through the throats of their sleeping children and his mulatto mistress before severing the reverend's own head—slowly, they say— with a handsaw.

Deborah Hardy, the woman who ran wild, stealing hens, crouching blood-caked in the branches of the orchard trees, wailing on moonless nights, killing hounds, shitting on the altar of her dead husband's church...

* * *

The shortcut runs through all that's left of the orchard, a few dozen bony trees laid out in a fading grid. This orchard once stretched for miles and is the location of the last reported sightings of Deborah Hardy after her change, a half-beast woman, pouncing on deer like a puma, hands curled like talons, face bearded in dried, black blood.

A dog barks in the distance. A chill wind blows through these remnant boulevards of trees.

We pass the maintenance shack, the stacks of split wood, tender bundles casting splinter-sharp, fingery shadows in the light of the house.

The fire escape, a straight metal staircase, angles down from the second-floor lounge into the gravel parking lot just past the shack.

A tread of raised teeth digs into our soles as we climb. We push back the square emergency door and climb over the sill into the lounge.

The television faces the wall, its screen probably still coated in ketchup, thick strands of aluminum foil hanging from the ceiling.

The inflatable man sits naked on the couch, his erection purple-headed, absurd.

You lunge at him, land a good punch in the face, then an uppercut, sailing him across the room.

My kick catches the blow-up doll behind the head, knocks him against the corner of the television's cabinet, where I punch him in the kidneys, his body folding at the impact.

Then we head downstairs.

* * *

Tegan's on the kitchen counter, her legs folded over and around each other in some pretzel yoga pose, eyes shut, humming a familiar tune.

She rotates a bowl of cereal in one hand, squeezing chocolate syrup over it with the other, syrup in tight circles, to the theme of some public service announcement.

Eddie stops us in the doorway, holds a hand up over his mouth.

You hold your hands up over your eyes.

I hold my hands up over my ears.

"She's focusing her samsara," he says. "Clearing away the static. Praba-something? Prama? I forget the exact terminology. And that's a great hat, man."

"Liquidation sale," I say. "Why is she humming *Play it Safe with Scissors*?"

"It's that one about garbage disposals, man. I can't remember what it's called, but you know it. There's that great line about fingers…"

"Oh, right," you say. *"Danger in the Kitchen."*

> *Disposal blades gnawing bone*
> *how the sound lingers.*
> *You'll never be able to dial the phone*
> *you've lost all your fingers.*

Eddie has a set of thin bar magnets duct taped to his wrist, polarized ends sticking out under his palm and above his knuckles.

"What's with the magnets, Yoder?" I say.

"The primary characteristics of the earth," he says. "Attraction and repulsion, a locked cycle of contrasting desires. Ancient Chinese medicine. I'm channeling orgones through bone."

"Your cyst again?" I say.

"Don't be reductionist, Wheeler. I'm talking about primordial homeopathy. This is bigger than the cyst. This is my new favorite drug."

"The cyst is actually getting pretty big," you say.

"And just wait till you see what I can do with cutlery."

Tegan's syrup bottle starts to burp, squirting out chocolate in bursts. She knocks it with her hand, gets another loose liquid blast, then the bottle goes dry.

She stops humming and unfolds her legs, letting them hang in their striped yellow-and-black tights from the edge of the counter. She wiggles her toes, one sticking from a rip in her tights, red polish on the nail.

Her eyes are red, too, when she opens them, red right where the black mascara starts, bigger than usual, frightened and sleep-sick, sunk deep in their smeared makeup frames.

She says, "The adult male California sea lion is between six feet, seven inches and eight feet, two inches long, with a weight of, on average, between 440 and 860 pounds."

"We've been reading a certain hunting and tagging manual," says Eddie. "Tegan's full of fun facts on our sea lion friends."

"Not my friends," she says. "I hate them, the whole bloated species, vulgar and fat, big wallowy worms covered in hair."

"But a very fine hair," says Eddie. "Fine and oily. Organic torpedoes, those creatures. Designed like living kayaks."

You pull out a cigarette, take a silver lighter from your jacket pocket. "How sweet, kiddo. 'To Kim, My One True Flame.'" You flip back the lid, suck fire till you can breathe smoke.

Tegan looks down at the empty syrup bottle, hands it to Eddie. "You can make a bunny bong," she says. "There'll be that, at least. One nice thing."

"How you holding up, T?" you say.

"He's stopped breathing five times," she says.

"Yeah," you say, "But he didn't stop breathing long enough."

"I'm just really pretty overwhelmed right now," says Tegan. "I mean, I'm mad at him, and I'm scared for him, and I'm scared for me, and I'm mad at me for not being more mad at him, and scared that I'm so scared, and… Oh, guys. I'm very much *not* grounded. I need a few hugs."

She puts the bowl down, and you wrap your arms around her, rock her back and forth. You step back, leaning your forehead against hers.

"So you gave meditation a try," you say. "Now maybe it's time for a more traditional Midwest family therapy, something liquid, huh?"

She pulls a crumpled soft pack from under the right epaulet of her old Russian army turtleneck sweater, sighs, reaches over to the range. She lifts up the cover, leans over and lights her cigarette on the blue pilot.

Her hair is short, Black Cherry #16, as is part of her forehead and the back of her neck. Charms hang from some of the bigger hoops in her ears: A skull, a dagger, a pair of ballet slippers.

"Drinks, kiddo?"

I check the refrigerator: Two cans of diet pop, a big jug of pineapple juice, a jar of curry paste, a plastic lemon, some salad dressing bottles, and a bowl of assorted fast-food condiment packets.

There are three empty ice trays and an empty box of tofu ice cream sandwiches in the freezer. The only thing in the cabinets above Tegan's head is a box of granola bars, the surface of which has yellowed with age.

Eddie says, "The liquor's hidden, man. This is Hardy House, remember? The apache quarter of campus. Straddling that fine line of the law."

"Where can a girl find a drink around here, T.?"

Tegan squints her eyes, rocks back and forth, sucking her cigarette like a pacifier, smoke puffing out her lips even as she drags.

"The red room," she says. "Send the boys."

She picks up the bowl again, begins to mix the syrup with the cereal. She holds her cigarette in one hand as she licks her other hand's gooey fingers.

"I really want you to try these muddy corn flakes, Courtney. We had to make them back in middle school, in home economics class. It's the *only* thing I can cook."

You take the bowl, ball up some of the mix with your fingers. You lick at it, then stuff it into your mouth and chew.

Tegan smiles with half her mouth, her eyes still sunk in worry. "What do you think?" she says.

"You can really taste the chocolate," you say.

* * *

I follow Eddie through the front sitting room, the portraits in their heavy frames, coal-black backgrounds, faces spot-lit, pallid and pasty with a varnished glow.

The brass State Historical Society plaque is propped on the mantelpiece, under an old, hand-stitched reproduction Viet Cong flag from the sixties: Red, a yellow star.

The house has been college property since the

founding, dating back to the religious days, home of the school's first president and home of his successor, the honorable Reverend Delmore Hardy, pastor, publisher, abolitionist. Hardy House was an administrative building till the fifties, when it became a frat house, then it was sold to a student co-op in the late sixties. The FBI raid came in seventy-one, a search for supposed stockpiles of hand grenades and sniper rifles for use by Cleveland Black Panthers. In the eighties the place was repeatedly slated for demolition, but students campaigned for status with the Historical Society, some alumni came out in force, including a state senator and a one-time Marxist Party presidential candidate. The preservationists placed some phone calls to Congress, and the plaque went up. Since that time the administration has done just enough repair work to keep Overflow Eight from being officially condemned, begrudgingly accepting the Class of 1969's gift of their Viet Cong protest flag in a ceremony at last year's Homecoming.

In Reverend Hardy's study, a down of frothy, fallen plaster coats the pool table, its green felt nicked in strips like cat scratches, thick slabs of yellow foam sticking up from the slit couch cushions.

Eddie knows the catch better than I do, the right amount of pressure, one solid knock to the upper right hand corner of the left panel on the south wall. There's a muffled sound as the spring releases, and the panel pops loose an inch or so. Eddie kneels down, grabs the small handle that swings out near the floor. He gives it a hard tug, leaning his weight into it till the panel slides back into the wall with a grind of metal against metal. I step through first, feel for the big square-cell flashlight, flick it on. Eddie pulls the door shut behind us, locks the catch back in place. We stand shoulder to shoulder on the landing, stone steps descending to the secret basement room, ladder rungs running up the barn-red walls, and we climb up to the hidden room at the south end of the attic, a safe haven from the underground railroad days, a chance for rest and healing before the final border run.

Eddie's hamming up the occult scene, saying "Deborah? Deborah, we're coming up. You decent?" Then, in a crypty falsetto, "Oh, Eddie, you know you can always come up and see me. And, *hello*, who's this? Are you bringing me a gift? Young man, young man, that is a *delicious* hat. If my husband had worn a hat that sexy, I wouldn't have had to hack off his head."

"Shut up, Yoder."

At the top of the ladder there's a pulley tied against the wall, and we step around it, into the room itself, a wooden steamer truck covered with candles, a Ouija board on the floor, the tall bong Wollinski pulled from the blaze.

A coiled sleeping bag rests in one corner, a box I recognize as one of Eddie's fire-survival kits, probably canned food and long underwear, maybe a duplicate copy of *The Middle of the Country*.

On the wall, further shadowed by a thick wood frame, hangs Deborah Hardy's age-darkened portrait, cracked canvas and a kind of glowing silhouette, gray pearl buttons up her pale starched collar, hair stretched back in a tight, silver bun.

Eddie pats the part of the canvas with the portrait's hand. "Next séance, man, you have to come. She's chatty. She sometimes speaks in rhyme."

"Let's just get the liquor and go."

He makes a ghost noise, brings up two bottles. "We have bourbon and we have rum. Should I mix you one? A half-and-half?"

"I guess Tegan's the one who needs it. What's she take?"

"Green tea. Echinacea. Ginkgo. I don't know. You want bourbon or rum?"

"Rum's more of a summer drink," I say. "Tropical times. Photosynthesis, sweat, the grit of sand."

"Can't confuse our seasons. Bourbon for fall, is it? Virgin white-oak barrels, the mellowing effect of char and time."

"Hell, bring 'em both. A half-and-half sounds great."

* * *

There are broken pieces of bowl on the floor by the doorway, a streak of chocolate syrup, thick with cornflakes, splattered across the kitchen wall.

You sit across from Tegan at the table, pushing a steak knife through the back of the syrup bunny, wiggling out a rough hole.

Tegan has her head in her hands, running her fingers through her hair, across her Black Cherry #16 scalp.

You say, "And I still hold on to this fantasy, I guess, tracking her down again, Alaska or California or wherever, of just being able to *talk* to her. This fantasy of her not being that crazy woman I visited at the place outside Columbus, the thick plastic wall between us, the little holes for sound. When she waved, T… the *blood*. Biting her fingertips open, gnawing wounds. That was before the mittens. I never saw her in the mittens."

Tegan notices me and Eddie in the doorway, gives us a quirky smile.

Eddie says, "How's a whiskey and rum sound? Can I mix you one?"

"Courtney thinks I should eat first."

You reach over and put your hands on hers, squeezing her clunky rings.

"She hasn't eaten since yesterday, guys. Shouldn't she eat?"

"But she just fixed up a batch of dirty cereal," says Eddie, taking a broom from the closet, beginning to sweep the broken chunks of bowl into a corner.

"Muddy," says Tegan, "Dirty cereal is the stuff they sell at sex novelty stores. Puffed rice shaped like little bla-blas."

"Eddie, take the girl to get some food. There's nothing here but stale granola bars and single-serve packets of mild salsa."

"Yoder might have some canned food stashed in the red room," I say.

"Jinx," he says, crossing himself in the shape of a jagged lightning bolt. "I've warned you before, Wheeler: Don't fuck with the fire."

"Guys, guys, don't *talk* about fire," says Tegan. "The squirrels are nearly through that wall over there, but I can't deal with anything else right now."

"T., have a drink," you say. "Then Eddie'll drive you out to the Amish Kitchen. There's pineapple juice to mix with, Eddie. Vitamins, T. Vitamins and alcohol."

"Oh, guys, guys. I'm just not dealing. My boyfriend's sleeping like a fairy tale and I'm scared and tired and hungry and I have chocolate syrup all over my sweater."

"Just let it out, T. It'll be ok."

"But what if it isn't?"

Eddie mixes up the rum and pineapple juice with the handle of a spatula from the sink. He hands the cup to Tegan, stands behind her, kneading her shoulders.

"Thank you," she says. "Thank you all. You're good. Oh, don't look at me. Please. I just don't want to cry. I hate that. How stupid. Crying."

"But it's ok," you say. "We can tell you've been crying."

"It's called makeup, Courtney. Something girls do."

She takes a sip, then tilts the cup back, finishes off the drink.

"That's the Tegan Bradshaw I know," you say.

"I just liked him so much better when he *breathed*."

Eddie crosses back to the counter to make more drinks. He stands by the sink, letting a chain of forks and spoons dangle from his wrist.

"Tricks with cutlery," he says. "I told you." As he turns toward us the bond breaks, silverware clattering and scattering across the linoleum.

"Eddie's been playing with those magnets for hours," says Tegan. "Ever since he found them in Bear's closet."

"And my energy levels are up," says Eddie. "I'm breathing deeper, able to concentrate more clearly."

"But," says Tegan, "It's too early to know if it'll really help with that impotency problem."

"Let's see how it works on your piercings, smart ass."

"Which ones?" she says.

She sticks out her tongue, but pulls it in again before Eddie can try. He taps his wrist against her ear, but nothing happens.

"No go, huh? Maybe they're aluminum or something. What do I know about magnets? Bear's the geology guy."

"And he's out like a rock," says Eddie.

He taps me on the shoulder, and the magnets hit bone. I pour two stiff whiskey and pops, hand one to you.

"You drinking, Eddie?"

"I'll pass. I'm wary enough of the Amish Kitchen. I want to face it sober. I hear they even brew their coffee in animal fat."

"But they also have tea," you say. "A nice cup of hot tea. Not so *common*. It's the civilized drink."

You wrap your arm around me from behind, pull me close to you.

"Sounds like a private joke," says Eddie. "Our cue to leave."

"All of this will be a private joke one day," says Tegan. "We'll see each other across campus and make seal sounds. We'll all have a good laugh. Unless we're too busy with the next crisis. Private jokes are kind of a luxury like that."

"Pain exchanged through personalized irony," you say.

"Speaking of private jokes," says Eddie. "It's Tuesday, right? Has anybody heard from Brandon?"

"He's killing himself again," I say.

"At least Kim knows the rules," says Tegan, "The pattern. Their scene is always the same, repeating."

You lean your head against my shoulder.

"Can I use your phone?" says Eddie. "I screened a call earlier from my sister's ex-boyfriend, up in Cleveland. He seemed kind of distraught. I almost picked up the phone then."

"Sure," says Tegan. "I better go check on Bear, anyway. That kid who works tech crew for the dance shows is up there now. We have to run a rotation, keep him from choking on his own tongue."

"We have to get going, too," you say.

You finish your drink, wink at me.

"How about maybe trying to keep up with me tonight, kiddo?" you say.

* * *

We take the long way back to your place, walking down the arched spine of the street, staying just shy of the shifting shadows, molting trees.

Leaves scuttle around in arcs and cursive loops, skimming off the concrete, rattling along the borders of dark lawns, cars' glass opaque with cold.

You turn to me, holding on to my arms, the blue of your eyes flushed steel gray by the night. Steam rises from inside your body. We shiver together.

"Catch me," you say.

And, like that, you turn, and you go, the slap of your boots on the concrete, fringe whirling like streamers. You swing your arms in front of you like a fighter.

We race past the steam plant's stack, the baseball field, the sleepy porch lights of professors' houses, the dumpsters in the cafeteria's loading dock, west down College, dueling bass beats throbbing between Overflow Two and Four, the buzz of distant, curtained mingling.

Some kid is taking a piss against a wall of the security headquarters. There's the throb of a strobe light, female laughter from a window of the big first-year dorm.

We slow before we reach the intersection with Wayne, the street lamp dead, the swinging traffic signal flashing blasts of yellow.

You run to the gutter and kick through a thick pile of dry leaves, then run back at me, tossing a fistful in my direction.

Weightless, they fall where they leave your hands, but you rush on, bump against me, press your cold cheek against mine, panting.

We hug each other close in the night, and you put your lips to my ear to speak. Something hard jams against my ribs.

"Ow," I say.

You step back, pull a bottle out from inside your jacket.

"I liberated the whiskey. Figured we needed it, to deal with our own sleeping lovers. I'm afraid of losing my touch, kiddo. I don't know how to talk about things in pretty ways anymore."

"Maybe it's better that way," I say.

"Not to say what you think. To come close to how you feel."

"I don't know," I say.

"There's such confusion with words."

"At least we're talking pretty again," I say. "We're not saying anything, but it sounds nice."

"I really want him to come," you say. "I really want him to come, and he won't, which makes me want him to not come, to never come, which makes me think that maybe that's what I already feel all the time, and that his *not coming* will just be a relief, that I want him to just be gone and out of my life."

"But to do his own going," I say.

"Exactly," you say. "Because I don't know how."

* * *

The laundry room is the warmest place in your house, four industrial dryers lining the west wall, shiny silver tubes snaking up behind them, soft foil, jointed with pie-pan metal elbows.

There are two washers against the opposite wall, and an ironing board, foam sagging under its floral cover, leaning against the vending machines of candy and condoms.

You cross to the sink on the far wall, the double basin gray with grime and dye. A tap squeaks open. You rinse out a plastic tumbler.

"I don't think they use it for bleach," you say. "Not that a little bleach ever hurt anybody."

You walk back to me, hand me the cup, its bubbly sorority letters nearly obliterated, scraped into fingernail-thick strips. You take out the bottle, pass it to me.

"Mix it up, kiddo."

"Double?"

"You don't have to get me drunk, you know."

"You're already drunk, Courtney."

"You've never *seen* me drunk. I just mean... Oh, never mind."

You twist the wire tie off a plastic bag full of octagonal orange plastic tokens, take one out, press it against your lips.

"We'll share," you say.

You feed the token into the machine's slot, shove the lever, hard, then pick your setting, start the spin.

"Any change?" I say.

"Never, kiddo. You should know that about me. I'm resistant. Entrenched."

"For a *pop*, Courtney. Quarters? Coins?"

"Just kick it," you say. "Right under the money place."

You take your cigarettes and Kim's lighter out of your pockets, hang your jacket from a blue peg above the sink.

You flatten your palms against the dryer's metal lid, lift yourself up onto it. There are gold-stitched chevrons on the back pockets of your jeans.

"Ah," you say. "Heat. Vibration."

I turn to the pop machine, give it a tentative kick. No response. I step back, try again with a hard charge, banging it back against the wall. A can drops.

"Iced tea, lemon flavor. How do we get something else, Courtney?"

"It only gives you one kind when you kick it," you say. "So pour a double. It's not like being drunk will hurt anything. And come over here, kiddo. Sit by me."

"I'm mixing our drink, Courtney."

"You say my name more when you're drunk."

"Courtney," I say.

I carry the tumbler over to you, let you mix the drink with your fingers. You take a sip, add another long, gurgling pour of whiskey, stir some more.

You hold your dripping finger up to me, slip it into my mouth, let me suck off the strong whiskey taste, a touch of sweet tea.

"It makes me feel guilty," you say, "The way you use my name."

"You want to remain anonymous?"

"I want to be someone else."

The dryer shakes, warm to the touch. There's a shift of gears beneath you, a kick as the spin slows.

"What is this?" I say, "Fluff cycle?"

"Permanent press."

I climb up next to you, and you scoot closer to me, wrap your arm around me.

"So why do you want to be someone else, Courtney?"

"I don't. It was just something to say."

"You are drunk, Courtney."

"Really, I mean it, stop with *Courtney* everything. There's just two of us here."

"Ok," I say.

"Alright," you say. "Here. Drink more. You're not drinking as fast as I am."

"I'm drinking, I'm drinking."

"A little local," you say. "Something for the pain."

"Courtney," I say.

* * *

I pretend to study the patterns of mildew streaking across the far wall, the way long lines follow the paths of leaks, the clumps of gray and pink lint along the floor.

And you take another drink, leaning back to swallow, those sinews in your neck, the blue vein running up and along your chin.

Eyes closed, you hand the tumbler to me, lean against my shoulder. The highlights of your hair shift and fall forward, bands of color, blonde on blonde.

There is the shutter-shaped blue membrane of your eyes, light hanging in crescent-curved squares, testing the edge of the depth of your pupils.

We stare into and beyond each other, the sound of spinning beneath us. When we feel most like touching, we take another drink.

"I should probably get going," I say.

"Where?"

"Home. To bed."

"To check your answering machine? A little late-night wallow in guilt?"

"To *sleep*. It's late. I'm tired."

"You know, you could always just pick up the phone when it rings. You'd have fewer messages to deal with that way. And I'm certainly not saying that out of sympathy for *her*, but because it pains me you refuse to address anything about your own life."

"You don't want me to use your *name*, but *I'm* the one hiding from my life?"

"Oh, don't, Martin. You know what I'm talking about."

"You're a mean drunk, Courtney."

"Maybe I'm just mean."

"Maybe you're just bitter."

"And why would that be? Because everything about love is a lie?"

"Nice one. Very organic."

"Don't condescend to me. *Just bitter*. You're so damned sensitive and edgy about everything."

"We're both drunk."

"There is only desire," you say. "The desire for what once was, in the moment. Desire for that lost immediacy—the *then*, the *could have been*."

"You've stopped making sense."

"No. I'm sober and I'm clear. A fabric of moments. Everything I love about him, I mean, it's not based on *fantasies*, just glossed-over, idealized *memories*."

"Vague memories."

"But sharp, real, present. That's how memory works, kiddo. Vague memories is a redundant turn of phrase."

"Padhya and I remember a time when we were what we needed."

"Cheers. Sloan remembers me as much younger, when I believed in Weak Chin, before I had my naiveté surgically removed."

"When we were smaller, in a smaller world."

"Perfect. We hear each other. King of the Carnival. Small in a small world. Now one of us needs to say something about dead ends."

"What do you remember about Sloan, then?"

"That's not fair, kiddo. That's not right."

"What do you mean? We were just—"

"This isn't the time. Don't taint things up. Just be. Us."

"Yeah," I say. "This will be one of our moments."

"Knee to knee," you say. "The warm rumble, two spare cinder blocks in the corner, the stale, linty exhaust smell."

Moist heat like an iron's steam. The liquor floating on your lips.

"We will say, 'Remember? It was fall.' And then good, strong, lyrical things, the weather, a sense of place, that these were easy, good, and too-little savored times."

"Ah, Courtney."

"This spark of authenticity, this is what we spend our lives longing for, kiddo, and we work at all these stupid, failed and failing relationships, and all we ever want is just to bring these moments back."

"But this isn't love? I mean, that isn't?"

* * *

The steel snap of Kim's lighter. You start another cigarette.

You say, "Tegan was right. Or Eddie. Whoever. Private jokes. That's all we have to look forward to. Postcards at the holidays, a phone call every six months, this coded exchange where nostalgia has been dulled to the level of cliché. They won't be *reminiscent* of anything, you know? They'll just be these things we say that remind us of all the other times we've said them. We'll laugh because it will be all that's left of a connection between us. 'Let sleeping seals lie.' Cue laugh track."

"Personal clichés," I say, "Their nostalgic value."

"That's a nice little idea. All fattened up by sleight-of-hand with words."

"You were the one philosophizing," I say.

"Relax, kiddo. I didn't mean anything, I was just quoting again. I'm trying to be more, well, what's it called? When you're referential, but not to yourself?"

"The opposite of Christ-like, apparently."

I am holding your hand at the wrist, your guitar strings pressing against my palm. There is nothing for me to say, so I just keep holding your hand this way, and you keep smoking.

You say, "There's a message from him upstairs. The father of my dead child. It'll be a good excuse, nothing I can argue with. Rudy didn't loan him the van after all, or there's some show he has to play, or..."

"There are probably six or seven messages from Padhya back on my machine. I mean, not all messages, but hang ups, too. She waits for the machine to come on, then hangs up, just so we'll know."

"Padhya's neurotic. You could do so much better."

"What kind of thing to say is that? *Do better.* What's that have to do with anything?"

"Always the promise of coming out, always saying he's thinking about maybe shopping for a ring."

"Why do we keep talking about them, though?"

"Our absent loves."

"Really, Courtney. There's something. I just wish we weren't drunk."

"We're just scared," you say. "What's that line from Patchen? 'We talked of things but all the time we wanted each other.'"

Threadbare, milk-pale denim, the full, warm roundness of a thigh.

"Patchen's a little clichéd, don't you think?"

"I wonder if that's even a quote."

"It's impressive, all this quoting."

"It's all for you. I constantly strive to impress you, kiddo. I just wonder where I heard it. There must have been something on television, because I never read."

"You either?" I say.

"I just can't, kiddo. My dirty little secret."

"You're illiterate?"

"Don't be dumb. I'm serious."

"You're not illiterate."

"Of course not. I just can't *read*. You know what I mean."

"Yeah. I know exactly what you mean. Look at me," I say. "My nervous system is in perfect working order. I'm capable of feeling."

"And I'm *capable*... That's a good one, kiddo. Sloan wouldn't get it. Kim wouldn't get it."

"Padhya would object to the phrasing. She'd have something clinical to say. 'Perfect working order' isn't a physical state. She weeds through everything I say, throws out the poetry."

You say, "Perfect working order is not a physical state."

"Too much," I say. "Too deep. Let's just drink and not talk."

"Martin, we're sophomores in college. This is the end of philosophy. From this point on, everyone we know will get old. We'll all take jobs involving impatient commutes and pink while-you-were-away memos. The skin under our chins will go soft and droop. Money will crush us. There will be never be time or humor enough. Our hair styles will look stupid in old photographs, and we'll be ashamed of our spinning dances, the lyrics of punk songs, that we ever drank wine with screw tops or did homework high on diet pills shoplifted from K-mart."

"Courtney. Drink. You don't know what you're talking about."

"Listen to me, Martin. One day we will look back on this and it won't be funny, and it won't be nostalgic. It just won't be anything. *We won't understand*. All real emotions die," you say.

"Remember the smell of those fat kindergarten crayons? Remember fireworks, or presents, anticipating everything? Remember how mirrors were special, or jinxes, or how sometimes, at night, the carpet of your bedroom would swarm with sharks? Right, you blush, you try to smile it away, that thing at the foot of the bed, but it was real, and now it's gone. We used to *believe*. Dreamy, dumb, white-trash kids sniffing correction fluid and talking about art. One day we'll be sorting through our papers, alphabetizing our old bills, and we'll come across a piece of our most real poetry..."

"Courtney," I say. "We're here. Now."

"Everything will be so clichéd, really."

* * *

Your cigarette is burning, is half gone. I watch the tip of it as you lift it to your lips, the fire as you inhale, the ash as it grows.

You pull as if you could take away more than burnt flavor and a vague buzz. You wrinkle up your nose, shielding your eyes with their own skin as paper and tobacco replace themselves with gray. The substance becomes intangible, a network of dust. You flick your fingers and it disappears.

You squeeze my hand in yours, biting down on your lower lip.

* * *

With a rapid ticking behind us, the dryer's engine stops. Something clicks shut inside the machine, although the spin continues for a minute or so, slower, slower, until, finally, there is nothing. The heat begins to fade, and the cold closes in upon us. You shiver, take your hand off mine and twist toward me, reaching past to grind your cigarette against the wall.

You leave a charcoal-black mark on the concrete, then field strip the butt, slicing the filter paper with your thumb nail, letting the last loose tobacco shake free.

You flick the tar-stained filter behind the next dryer, take the bottle, tilt it back, and pass it to me. You press the bottle to my lips, force me to drink.

You say, "*I live here*, officer. Let me into the kitchen."

My fingers move across the curving folds of your ear, into and through your warm, smoky hair, close to the scalp, cupping the roundness of the back of your skull.

"Courtney," I say. "I mean…"

And my lips are touching your hair, and you are whispering into my ear, my arms around you, your breasts pressing hard against my chest, your thighs against mine.

"There's no good way to say this yet, kiddo."

"But I want you," I say, or start to say. You interrupt.

You keep your eyes open, lead with your tongue, a sudden heat, strong as a shot of whiskey. You make a sound of surprise as you lean farther against me.

You bite down on my tongue and pull me closer, your hands fanning out, kneading across my limbs, over my chest, working a gap in my shirt as you taste my molars.

I push back, wrapping around you, your open eyes curling up in a smile, another noise rising out of you, this one settled, past shock, into pleasure.

You straddle me on the dryer, my hands hard against your ass, the moist, hot denim between your thighs, sliding under the waist of your jeans, that triangle of panty in back.

You pull up your shirt, guide my face down to the skin of your belly, your belt buckle against my cheek, a hand down the back of my shirt, a hand kneading at my crotch.

The shelf above the washer begins to rattle, a detergent scoop shaking loose and falling to the floor.

"The stairs," you say, pulling away.

On my tongue is the taste of the silk underside of your bra, but you are standing on the ground now, clothes straightened, knees bent, ready for impact.

"Sloan," you say.

* * *

You say, "You're early."

"I thought I'd surprise you, babe."

"You did."

"I just couldn't wait. Drove straight over here just as soon as I got the keys."

"A real surprise."

"It's a fancy place, this college."

"I guess."

"No, it's pretty, all the lights, the pathways."

"Sometimes."

"I hope that gravel lot back there's ok. I mean, I left the van—"

"It's fine," you say.

"I *can't* get towed. It's the bakery van. Rudy let me borrow it because I hooked him up with some really good—"

"It won't get towed," you say.

"You look good, babe."

"Yeah?"

"Yeah."

You do not keep photographs of your lover, at least not out in the open. So I have never seen him before, but all the same, he is what I expected, tall, with a simplified face, like a character from a comic book, a face reduced to its main lines and painted a flat, fleshy salmon, broad, a strong chiseled nose and chin.

He wears an old shooting jacket over his flannel, a quilted shotgun pad on the shoulder, elastic shell loops above the big front pockets where he keeps his hands as he shifts back and forth.

He keeps his head low, looking up at you with his eyebrows, face cocked to the side, leading out with that smooth, square chin.

"So," he says. "This is where you live."

"Well, this is the laundry room, but I spend some time here, yeah."

"Who's the guy?"

"The guy. This is Martin. Martin Wheeler, Sloan, etc., whatever."

"Martin. I've heard about you."

A big, calloused hand, a hard shake, like he's trying to snap the bones of my wrist. I step back, fish my hunting cap out of the gap between the dryers, put it back on my head.

"I'm sure it's mutual," you say. "Say something, kiddo."

I say, "Yeah. Hey. Good to finally meet you."

"You, too," he says, but he's on you now, breathing across your face. He says, "Babe, babe, all this way. Don't I get a couple kisses, don't I deserve *something*?"

* * *

So I go home.

Eddie's not here yet. I can't face the answering machine alone.

That dose of diet pills and generic ephedrine substitutes has jolted my heart into a new, quick-time rhythm, the industrial remix of physiology.

Either the pills or the taste of your tongue, that hard, pulsating pressure of your lips against mine.

Blinking, blinking, blinking.

Alone in a room with an evil red robot eye.

And my lips are sore from you. You are that good.

I still have the campus paper I took from Language Housing, so I sit down on my bed in my shoes and my clothes and my hunting cap, and I read it.

A high school Nazi gang is suspected in a recent rash of vandalism.

A first year student from Pasadena is in the hospital with a concussion, internal hemorrhaging, and two cracked ribs.

A sophomore physics student has discovered a new star.

At the BioScience research station there's a calf with a Plexiglas window in its stomach, a pig with a mechanical heart.

The visiting chemistry professor is conducting research on the psychedelic properties of certain Northern Ohio lichen.

The chapel was broken into last week, some Easter banners defaced, a communion chalice and several candlesticks stolen.

Omens abound.

By the time I reach the sports page, the items refuse to remain separate, distinct. Astrological insights are concealed in the football scores, the distances between cosmic bodies, giant ruby-studded mushrooms, a church hung with swastika banners, a cow eviscerated on the altar, its intestines dragged down the aisles by masked townies, but still alive, eyes like wet marbles, thick tongued, moaning...

* * *

Eddie's shaking me awake, saying, "Don't *you* pull this sleep shit on me."

I bat him away. "It's night," I say. "I'm supposed to be asleep."

"Wheeler, you are wearing shoes and a hunting cap in an extraordinarily gaudy color designed specifically to keep you from being accidentally shot while wandering the woods in camouflage. The lights are on, you're on top of the covers, and there's broken answering machine all over the middle of the floor. I am entirely unconvinced that this is standard sleeping procedure. I find it fairly disturbing. I think you should be *awake*."

He's holding a black plastic panel in his hand. The internal pieces are still strewn out in a rough line across the floor, like the wreckage of a plane crash, plastic shards, those soldered cards with little bumps and hooks and microprocessors, something that was maybe once a speaker.

The tape case has been cracked open into two matching sides, disemboweled, the tape itself trailing from my bed to the far window like a glistening parasitic worm.

"I don't remember the answering machine," I say.

I lie back down on the bed, cover my head with my hands.

"I don't remember that at all."

"You're a little drunk, man. I'm inferring that, working with some obvious clues. Sorry I woke you up, but we need to talk."

"Ok. I'm awake. I'm lying down, the room is shifting rapidly at fairly pronounced angles, but I'm awake. What do we need to talk about?"

"I need you to ride up to Cleveland with me tomorrow."

"Why?"

"Tegan wants us to drive Bear up to his parents' house, and my sister's ex-boyfriend needs to me haul a llama corpse up to his studio in Coventry."

"I have class tomorrow," I say.

"But you only have a morning class," he says. "And you hardly ever go to class, anyway."

"Did you just say something about a llama?" I sit up again, make a couple of attempts at untying my shoe laces.

"My sister's ex-boyfriend... You know the guy, the artist, calls himself Shivaji, all into ska, plaid, Boston accent."

"Three Short Films About Roadkill?"

"Yeah. And that installation you and I saw together. The sheep? On the ceiling?"

"I remember the guy, yeah. Hard to forget." I finally get the shoe laces undone, kick off my shoes, pull off my cap.

"So you're coming, right?"

"Did you say something about a *dead* llama?"

"Natural causes. There was a death at the llama farm, Shivaji got a call about it... People seem to know he's in the market for these kinds of things..."

"These kinds of things? You mean *dead animals*?"

"So they'll let him have it for free, but he doesn't have a truck. He has an Omni. And it'll start to rot soon, and—"

"And something about Bear, too?"

"Well, since we'll be going practically past his parents' house anyway, Tegan thought..."

"Why aren't there doctors involved in all this, again?"

"One more drug incident and everyone in Hardy House gets relocated by the housing office. Besides, Bear's parents are *veterinarians*. That's how he got into all this stuff in the first place."

"Yoder, I'm going to sleep. Just wake me up when everything is over. Tell me how I handled it all."

I roll over toward the wall, onto a sharp silver piece

from our former answering machine. I throw it at Eddie, then cover my head with my pillow.

* * *

I sink back into a repeating nightmare, staring off at the empty horizon, a vastness so barren it threatens to drink up everything.

Heaving swells, loud sound, the water all around, a living gray, impenetrable, a constant loop.

The ocean churns, pulsing dumb as static across a monochrome television screen, and I am a child again, with a child's anxiety, choking on the cold salt spray, the rumble from deep below, the low clouds, the close storm wind.

Everything folds in upon itself, crashing clockwork, a self-devouring machine.

I wade out into the writhing, dark rush of it, undertow scissoring around my legs, then I am swimming, held in a tepid envelope, dense liquid muffling my slow kicks.

Up, lifted on a hump, then the force of a froth wall as it shatters against my face, the first taste of brine and the sudden pull. Ducked under, up, then, with the next crest, plunged.

A moment passes with this first sense of warmth, embryonic security. Then there is the need to breathe. Time under becomes a sharp struggle, and I'm surfacing again, gasping for breath, skull pounding to that distant, thundering roll of surf.

Again, then again, crashed under, pulled down, this sound like tons of sand shifting. I'm spinning as I'm held down, struggling to move, if only to gesture, if just to contort my face in pain.

All my life I have had this dream, waking clammy with sweat and certain of suffocation.

I am watching the sky from underwater, flickering streaks and diamonds of haze-gray light, slow weight pressing me in a coffin, sunk currents moving things along their own dead, set paths.

* * *

I'm up with the first orange sliver of sun that slices through the plywood planking where our east window used to be.

Head throbbing, thirsty, I'm trying not to think about my girlfriend, still feeling the warm weight of your breast cupped in my palm.

Eddie's not here, must have gone back to Hardy House, though the answering machine pieces are laid out across his desk, ready for cannibalization at Kent.

I need a glass of water. Some coffee. A new life, free of these memories of Padhya's voice, her insistence masking frustration, like how she asks, "Before we graduate, right? We have to be engaged by then."

I head downstairs for a glass of water. Wollinski's in the kitchen, smoking over her journal.

"What are you doing up so early, Wheeler? You just get home?"

"I'm changing my ways," I say. "Starting this morning, I'm going to lead an honest life, disciplined, temperate."

"You're going to make it to class today?"

"I always make it to class."

"If by always you mean usually, and if by usually you mean make it there at ten, it being a nine o'clock class."

We walk over to the cafeteria together, Wollinski and I, for breakfast, which apparently is covered by our meal plan and served every weekday morning, though this is my first time.

The sun is bright, burnishing the hard air.

Wollinski says, "Is it true Tegan Bradshaw's getting expelled for talking about masturbation on the radio?"

"Maybe," I say.

The light makes my eyes ache, sinks a sharp pain to the back of my brain.

We climb the spiral staircase of the student center, past the posters for the fraternity blood drive, Friday's open mic, the next meeting of the Human Rights Club.

Wollinski's wearing a t-shirt from the School of the Americas, and when I ask if she got it from one of the protests, she doesn't understand what I'm talking about.

The cafeteria is nearly empty, just a few lone students reviewing notes for tests, a table of sorority girls with caps over their hair.

We stop by the salad bar first, loaded at this hour with fruit and Jell-O, a vat of purple yogurt, a basket of bagels and toaster pastries.

Wollinski claims a table by the back windows, gets herself a cup of hot tea. I go to the drink machines, fill up four glasses with orange soda.

We file through the line, sliding our still wet, machine-hot trays across the rail bar this side of the glass, the vats behind, slabs of German toast floating in their own grease, limp bacon, Spanish omelets oozing cold salsa and thick rings of black olives.

Bryce Gibson's working the line, a shower cap over his shaved head.

"You want a croissant, Odessa?" he says. "We got some in back."

"Thanks, sweetie," says Wollinski.

"You want one, Wheeler?"

"I'll just go for one of those pressed egg products," I say, pointing at the eerily yellow rolls of shiny omelet-like matter. Suddenly, I want to cry, remembering the way smoke slips up past your lips, how carefully you speak. And I'm thinking of Sloan, the angles of his big ears and how his Adam's apple, large and low, bobbed when he spoke. That pressure of him walking toward you, the way he hugged you from behind, rubbing his chin down on the top of your head. You were saying something to me, but then you just grunted and shut your eyes. And as I left, he grabbed you again, took your ass in his hands like he was handling a melon down at Zeisberger's, checking for ripeness, thumping and sniffing...

"I've never seen you at breakfast before," says Bryce.

"It was just *that* rough a night," I say.

"You look like you could use some coffee."

"Gibson, I can't fucking stand this life I'm trapped in, and I'm terrified of any other possibility. What I could use is another dozen drinks and a few years of solid, undisturbed, dreamless sleep. I want to wake up someplace where no one knows me, where no one speaks any language I know."

He pulls a pill canister out of his apron pocket, shakes a couple of blue and white capsules on my plate, next to the omelet.

"Have some anti-depressants," he says. "You want any home fries?"

"No, thanks. I'm good now."

"Is Tegan really in jail?" he asks.

"Yes," I say.

* * *

Wollinski and I take Landscape together every Monday, Wednesday, and Friday morning. The class spends the first half hour (which I almost always skip) in a conference room of the Art Center, our most recent pictures hung along the wall, everyone taking turns at hackneyed critiques.

Someone always says, "There's a definite expression of *feeling*," and someone else always says, "The foreground detail is really *good*." The girl in the knit cap says, "Maybe it's less realistic, but I *like* it," while Wollinski goes with "*Good* work with the balance of the scene."

"I *appreciate* your sense of distance," is my standard line, though I don't know if someone else claims it when I'm not there.

The next hour and a half is spent working from life.

Today we are spread out on the slope west of the Art Center, looking back toward campus across the oak grove, focusing on the stand of small, young trees along the Center's wall.

I sit with Wollinski on the crest of the hill, our backs against the college's long stone sign. She's trying pastels today, my tackle box set between us so she can share my colors.

The sky is a washed blue, the blustering wind knocking deep-wine leaves out of the trees, the hillside's long grass flashing in gentle waves under the glossy viewbook light.

The edges of my big sketchpad pages flip up and tear at the sides where I have them fixed in place with rusty metal clips.

Wollinski smokes as she works, wipes her fingers on the quilt patches sewn over the knees of her Army trousers.

There's a tart dampness to the autumn air, a taste like cider to the wind, the sun bright and strong on my face, making the page flash white.

I'm using the leaves of the big tree at the Center's edge as the left frame for my scene, a pure yellow spotted with the red of its neighbors, its trunk long and dark against the bleached stone blocks of the building. The grove's oaks enter my line of vision above the rise, with a curving strip of footpath behind them, and then Old Main's metal steeple, a chalky cornflower blue.

Wollinski's skewed the angle a little, putting the tops of the oaks just below the steeple, working closer in, trying to capture the rain-blackened grooves, the details of shade.

The wind comes through again, a rustled roar echoing around us.

Wollinski offers me a mentholated drag, and I accept, sucking quick and hard, a flaring singe of mint.

I say, "You know what Portraiture class did Monday? They took a trip to the nursing home. They made charcoals of an old woman on a respirator."

A pair of squirrels chase each other up the trunk of a tree, circling around, their claws making a sound like dry leaves as they scrape and catch in the crevice lines of bark.

Wollinski takes her cigarette back, finishes it off, examines the filter end and files it away in my tackle box of pastels, right next to sienna.

The squirrels have split up, one up in the branches, the other hanging upside down on the trunk. This hanging one looks at us, tilts its head to watch the other kids scribbling over their sketch pads.

Wollinski clucks her tongue, digs a rubber band-bound cellophane bag out from her left leg's cargo pocket, catches the squirrel's attention with the crinkle.

It scampers down from the trunk, stands up on its hind legs. It sniffs the air, then heads our way with high, arching, full-body leaps.

She shakes out a handful of pretzel chips, offers some to me. I have one. She has one. She clucks her tongue again and holds one out toward the squirrel.

"Tradition, Quality, and Great Taste," she says. "Wollinski Family Snacks: The Name You Grew Up With."

The squirrel stands stock still, watching. Another sniff, a hesitation, then a leap, another. It stops again about a yard from her feet, stands up on its back legs again.

She puts the pretzel chip on her thumbnail and flicks it like a tiddlywink. It lands in the grass in front of the squirrel, who jumps and has it.

The squirrel pops back up on its hind legs, turns the pretzel chip in its paws, takes a series of quick, tasting bites, then mouths the thing and bounds off toward the trees.

"Is it true about Bear?" she says. "He's in some kind of coma?"

"He's just asleep," I say. "He sent away for one of those mail-order air rifles, the kind with the tranquilizer darts for California sea lions. He shot himself in the foot for a high."

Wollinski turns back to the tackle box, lifts up the folding shelves again, searching through the more metallic tones.

She says. "Do you have a gold that's like really shiny, like with sparkles in it?"

"For a while I had some funky makeup down on that third tier," I say. "I had some sparkly lipstick I used a lot, all different colors."

"Yeah," she says. "Cool, I'll try this."

"It might be too bronze."

"No, bronze is good. I didn't mean gold. Why did I say gold?"

She pushes her glasses up, stares across at the roof, the cool, clear space, these aged hues, their fierce definition.

"My picture sucks," I say. "These leaves look a little *too much* like fire. But, how can you be expected *not* to get carried away?"

She looks over at my pad, puts her hand to her chin.

"There's a *definite* expression of feeling," she says. "Or a definite expression of *feeling*."

We have a nice laugh at that one. I eat another pretzel chip as she tests various sticks against the edge of her sketchpad.

"How do you get your hands on something like that?" she says. "I thought he was a Geology student. Does he work at Sea World in the summers or something?"

"His parents are veterinarians," I say. "And he gets all these catalogues: Pet supplies, zoo equipment, safari gear."

"Oh," she says. "Can I break this maize? I need a fine line."

"Sure. But I want that pine if you're not using it right now. No, the fat, round one."

"Oh," she says. "This one's great. It's so powdery."

"Yeah," I say. "It's really soft. And dark. It gets into the teeth of the paper, makes itself known."

She watches me make a few heavy slashes in the lower right corner, smudge them slightly, the shape hinting through, the wall of evergreens on the way to Administration.

I'm twisting my thumb down on the pigment, swirling it around like those wide, needley boughs shaking in the wind. I take a snapped piece of a deep ultramarine and add a few shadow flecks.

"So what's going to happen to him?" she says. "I mean, what kind of shape is he going to be in when he finally wakes up?"

"I haven't really given it any thought," I say.

* * *

A maze of roses at the arboretum half an hour south of town. Padhya and I went there once, kissing between the brambles, thorns a harder color than their stem's fresh flesh.

That was last fall, the season already stripping off the softer, less ready petals. The light low, like velvet, spongy grass sinking under our feet, a sharp wind in our faces.

We ate apples we bought from some roadside stand along the drive down.

Padhya had a ring catalogue inside her purse, a cousin just engaged, back in England, a year younger than her and—as she said at least three times—much prettier.

I lost track of her conversation, watching the way the wind battered back all these barbed plants, the arrow-shaped black heads that would never open, the blighted leaves spotted with violet and brown.

A few full, dimply, pink blossoms, the color of hard-packed cotton candy, petticoats inside petticoats: These were what I remembered when I woke the next morning to the thin, gray frost on the ground outside.

* * *

Eddie has a mug of lukewarm pineapple juice waiting for me at Hardy House, the side entrance propped with a wedge of firewood, the screen door slamming on its hinges after me.

Eddie's coloring his fingernails with a highlighter, sitting at the kitchen table, felt tip squeaking. He doesn't even look up at me, just gestures with his chin to the mug.

"Bear's awake," he says. "And he's *hungry*."

He blows on the nails of his left hand, biohazard orange. I sit down across from him, take a drink, pick a string of fruit pulp off my lip.

"He's moving really slow, and is, you know, kind of drowsy. But he's standing ok. He's been up maybe an hour, seemed to understand when I told him to get dressed and be down here by noon. Tegan's sleeping, finally, said she might sleep for days. You look better than when I last saw you."

He does a bit of touch up on his thumb, then rubs his cyst, starts coloring the skin around it with an orange bullseye.

"What he *really* needs is a bath. He smells pretty much like the shit he soiled himself with earlier this morning. But I don't want him to drown, and I don't want to help him out *that* much. Seeing him in his freaky leopard-print bikini briefs and knee-high hiking socks was traumatic enough. I've always known he was a hairy guy, but I never knew *how* hairy till today."

"That's interesting what you did with your nails," I say.

"It's open season. You've got that hat to protect you. I need something, too. You weren't there for the scene at the Amish Kitchen last night. There were all these bikers. Elderly folks. Christians. Some gang that tours the country, Bible verses on their leather jackets, handing out little pamphlets on salvation. Good Word Riders, or Good News, something *Good*, I think. Anyway, Tegan was crying, so all these geriatrics flocked around our booth. One woman gave her an angel pin, this, like, seventy-year-old woman in a leather bra, an entire nativity scene tattooed across her back. Camels and everything. They led a sing along, with the whole restaurant. Nobody knew any church songs, but we did 'This Land is Your Land.' Tegan and

I taught everybody the lost verses, and the bikers paid for our food. I think it made Tegan feel better, all that religion. These were compassionate people. Crazy, wrong, and frightening people, but caring in their own sugary, lug-nut way. They read something from *Jonah*, which seemed apropos enough. According to the Bible, they said, Tegan should dump Bear."

I'm staring over at the door to the bathroom, where a Good Touch, Bad Touch poster is tacked, a string of cartoons illustrating, in those avocado and almond tones of seventies kitchen appliances, the learned distinction between love and abuse.

"When you got back to campus," I say, "Did you meet Sloan?"

"Courtney's being anti-social with him. Tegan and I went over to Three, but she wouldn't open the door. They haven't left her bedroom since he got here."

Every memory of you is now flavored by physicality, our overlap of space, the hot width of your tongue probing deeper into my mouth, your teeth gritting against mine.

The curve of your knees, the shiver of your breasts. The bones that set and frame your hips. Folded funnels of ears. Delicate down of flesh-colored hair along your neck.

I'm trying to wrestle with this sudden solidity, with your firmness, your body as something responsive against mine, something real under my grip.

"I see you lost your magnets," I say.

He rubs his orange wrist, bends it a few times, taps on the swollen growth with the end of his highlighter.

"Gave them to an arthritic biker. But I think my cyst is already receding."

* * *

Eddie slides a copy of Shivaji McArthur's chapbook, *Sausage Processing and Other Poems*, across the table to me.

I open to a piece called "The Inside Story of Sandwich Meat," composed as a dialogue between the meat-grinding machine and the bonding agents that hold the reconstituted meat product together.

"That guy's one of the main reasons I became a vegetarian," says Eddie.

The pages are gritty and brown, like grocery bag paper. I flip around, skim the titles.

"Is this where you first heard of the USDA's Mind Control Hormones?" I say.

"As a matter of fact," says Eddie. "He found out about that stuff when he was still dating Cathy. They used to hang out with this ex-CIA agent, used to work in the dairy division."

"What are we doing about lunch?" I say.

"Tegan gave me Bear's wallet, which is kind of gross with all his recent teeth marks on it, but has more than enough money to buy us all some severe doses of homestyle country cooking. I figured, as hungry as he is, we should stop by the Moveable Feast."

"That's an ugly scene," I say.

"Which fits with the general theme. Besides, it'll give him a chance to test his reflexes, and it's on the way."

Eddie's wearing a sock cap, a long-sleeve sweatshirt advertising some punk band with a picture of a motorcycle crash.

"I stopped by the room this morning, by the way. The phone rang, and since there is no machine, I picked it up. Took me damn near twenty minutes to get off the line, and it wasn't like she was saying much, just sighing, asking about how busy we must be. She made me promise three times to tell you she called. Your girlfriend's *really worried* about you."

"So am I," I say. I'm staring at his shirt, the shiny, plastic appliqué of the helmetless man smearing himself across the pavement, the streak that used to be his legs stretching back to the horizon.

* * *

Fall Carnival is not Homecoming. It is an event far more Ohio, the candied excess of a church ice cream social out of hand, rustic as poison oak.

Fall Carnival functions as a sort of fund-raising street fair, except on those years when it rains. Then it becomes a sort of street fair inside a high school gymnasium.

Padhya and I arrived late that rainy night of our senior year. We missed the pie-eating contest, the apple bobbing, the dunk tank appropriated from some situation comedy.

We had been making out in her car. My fingers were in her cunt, the passenger seat fully reclined, out at one of the park's more remote turn-offs, coal truck lights occasionally glancing off the bleary, steamed glass.

The fight I only barely remember, and I don't remember if it started at the dance, on the way there, or even earlier, though this is the most likely, as our conflicts have always been slow in building.

Maybe this was one of the ones over college, Padhya mad that I wasn't applying to any of the schools she wanted to go to, not the ones in California, the one in Jersey, that place down south.

By the time we made it to the Carnival, she couldn't stop crying. She ran out of the gym, past the makeshift booths of baked goods, beeswax candles, hand-carved Santa Claus figurines.

She ran to the women's restroom across from the weight room, the janitor's closet, right in front of the iron accordion gates, locked across the corridor to keep wanderers out of the empty school.

And Ms. Harris, the typing teacher, and Mr. Gordon, from Algebra, sat in folding chairs stationed in front of the gate, their chairs close enough to touch, two chaperones sneaking a smoke under the framed Evils of Marijuana poster.

Padhya and I turn to this night so much, telling stories of this one, golden, good time, fabricating a memory to keep our present misery afloat.

But she came out of the bathroom screaming, saying how she hated the town, the people, their stupidity and small views. She said the worst thing her father ever did to her and her mother was to take a position in Ohio.

She was saying something else about her mother, sleeping pills, a threat of divorce, but then the lights went low and amber spots came up on the stage: The Queen was called.

Fall Carnival's Queen is crowned on the basis of having sold the most tickets to the Saturday morning pancake breakfast. The King is just whatever guy she chooses.

And Padhya still chose me, although even that was a desperate, default decision.

She dried her eyes and took my hand, and we climbed to the stage, led our dance. We got pictures taken, bought prints, both wallet-size and larger ones for framing.

We pretended to smile, pretended to kiss, until we pretended to believe in us again.

*　*　*

Hardy House has a mounting block by the curb, a horseshoe-shaped stone with a step inside it, worn down slick and steep, a step Deborah Hardy once used, raising her skirts for the climb into her horse-drawn carriage.

Ours is a less graceful routine, loading Bear into Eddie's pickup.

The boy's in bad shape. He can only speak in grunted, broken syllables, none of which come out in ordered sentences, most of which is gibberish anyway. He can't fully open his eyes or focus his vision, just squints, his mouth hanging open, drooling. His motor control is shot. He's twitching isolated muscle groups, tensing and kicking in spasms. He can only walk in very slow, measured steps, dragging his feet as if skating in slow motion. He's managed, somehow, to shower, though not to rinse, acidic-smelling blue shampoo caked in his hair.

Eddie keeps asking him if he slept well.

We lead him out to the curb, where Eddie's left his truck, which he bought off his uncle after his uncle bought it back from the insurance company after getting it totaled in a T-bone crash with a school bus. Eddie put some money into it, a new headlight, alignment, fresh tires, but he only fixed those elements essential for driving. There's a wooden plank for a back bumper, a web of fractures across half the windshield. The passenger side door doesn't open, and that whole side is smashed in, rusted.

So we have to push Bear in through the driver's side.

I climb into the cab, brace my feet on the seat and try to pull Bear in by his overall straps. Eddie's on the block, trying to lift Bear's legs, slide him in like a load of boards.

But Bear won't stay steady. His knees wobble out in opposite directions, bow back toward each other. His arm flaps up, hard, catching Eddie across the face.

Eddie falls back, off the block, and Bear slides out of the cab, slumping down into the mud. He's drooling even worse now, and his stomach growls.

"Did you say he shit himself earlier?" I say.

"Yeah. But he was still asleep at the time," says Eddie. "I hope he doesn't do it again. I think he's too big for the jump seat. He'll have to be up front. Sorry."

"That's alright," I say. "I'll be that much farther away from him."

Eddie gives a sort of grimace, then hoists Bear up by his straps again.

"Let's try again," he says, this time standing Bear up and tilting him forward, slamming him against the side of the truck.

I grab one of his arms, pull him down to the door, drag him inside. Once he's in, I climb over into the back, the driver's side jump seat, prop my feet on one of Eddie's fire-preparedness duffel bags.

Eddie hops into the front seat, manages to get Bear's seat belt snapped together just as Bear slouches back into sleep, straining against the strap, leaning down toward the dashboard. I grab his overalls at the point where the straps merge, lean him against the seat slowly, its plastic back swelling with his weight.

"Forgot to tell you," says Eddie. "He has trouble staying awake once he sits down."

The engine sputters up into a rough roar. Eddie lets it go for a while, gunning the gas.

Bear launches into a brothy snore, mucus catching in his throat on the inhale.

Then we pull away, leave behind Hardy House's sagging facade, the gloomy strips of blistered paint, the second-story shutter that hangs from a single hinge, and, behind the house, the dark brambles of the orchard, the bare trees scraping against the sky.

* * *

Heading down highways lined with hay bales, harvester paths ringing sloped fields with lines like those on contour maps.

An afternoon angle to the autumn light, shadows of grain silos and the wood wig cut-outs in front of the road-side beauty shop.

Gravel paths, cinder block foundations, and bare mud rectangles in the yard of the former used-RV dealership.

Cattle pastures' barbed wire, billboards for prayer. Russet leaves scatter across asphalt, scrolling back in our wake's draft.

This is not Ohio as John Glenn saw it, spiraling out, tether-bound, hundreds of miles above: The deepest-scored of scars, the clusters of paved acres and electric spires.

This is the land itself: Antique agricultural implements rusting in a gravel lot, the smoke-flavored roofs of barns caving in, flanks advertising extinct brands of pouch tobacco.

A soil accustomed to blood, flint chips and arrowheads peppering farmers' fields. Bed of the living Teays, brine-pickled stone skeletons of the broad-fingered river web: The Scioto, the Olentangy, the mighty Maumee pressing on like smelted steel under the bridges of Toledo. Cleveland, crouching at the charred gullet of the Cuyahoga, the lamprey-thick black lap of Lake Erie.

Shuttling forward along this two-lane country road, watching the yellow slashes as they disappear under the hood, propelled by the repetition of sounds back down to the solid heart of place, the horse-drawn buggy vending cider and johnny cake from the hillside of the turn-off to the Interstate.

* * *

Like a drive-through liquor store or a rifle loaded with recreational drugs, Mama's Homestyle Country Smorgasbord puts a premium on convenient access to its amenities.

This is the epitome of user-friendly service, a business moving to the customer's pace, and *moving*, too, perfect for Bear, for the random masses of the heavily sedated.

Here the buffet comes to the eater, vats of steaming food jerking forward on conveyor belts, rotating around the bars like luggage at an airport baggage claim.

The clientele of Mama's are, for the most part, lumpy, lethargic, tuber-like people, often in family groups, or at least groups that dress alike, often groups with name tags.

Every few feet the food pauses, and these people scoop out huge sluggish spoonfuls of chicken gizzards, pork gravy, fried okra, beanie weenies.

Two o'clock on a Wednesday afternoon, and there are crowds around the mechanical peninsulas, noses grinding against the sneeze-guards.

Armed with ladles and tongs and slotted serving spoons, a determination on their thick-set faces, these modern hunter-gatherers prepare to catch their food.

Eddie and I grab plates off the spring-loaded stack, or, rather, Eddie grabs a plate which turns out to be two stuck together, hands the second to me.

We take places in line at the vegetable trough, behind a wide-shouldered woman whose shirt back reads: MY OTHER ASS IS A SIZE SIX.

I ask Eddie if he knows what this means. He's shaking his head violently, his eyes squeezed tight.

Bear, slightly invigorated by the smell of so much low-quality food, shows some of his old strength. He doesn't bother with a plate or with standing in a line. He just shoulders aside some smaller eaters, plants himself under the pink neon "MEAT" sign, and then begins to shovel riblets, catfish nuggets, chicken wings, meat balls, shepherd's pie, roast beef, and sausage patties directly onto his tray.

"This is another one of those places where they fry the *soup*," says Eddie. "At the end of the day, I bet they mop the floor with beef drippings."

He hovers his head above the splattered rail of the bar, the chain of vats jerking back into the cave of the kitchen where they are restocked.

"It's like a very cholesterol-heavy train set," he says.

Two guys in cowboy hats walk up beside Bear. They take spatulas and start prying at the vat of catfish nuggets. They pull it up, water dripping from the underside, and carry it toward their table, a long one against the far wall, full of men and women in cowboy hats, who raise a cheer.

I say, "So we're just going to let him eat his fill, pay our bill, and then drop him off at his folks' place, as inconspicuously as possible."

"With one stop along the way to pick up a dead llama. And assuming that between now and then he doesn't fall asleep with a chicken thigh down his throat. But that's the plan, yes."

"Do you think his parents will notice a difference?"

"We'll say he's been overworked at school. Mineral testing, that big *tectonics* exam. He pulled one too many all nighters, so now he's fatigued, he's coming home for the weekend."

"It's Wednesday."

"For a *long* weekend. Look, this is a piece of cake. The main thing is that we just act natural, stick to our story, push through, pass everything off as cool."

"I know, I know. In the face of chaos, maintain."

Bear leans against the meat bar, snapping a pair of tongs just shy of the pork chops, which, with a rumble, shift along the line, out of range.

"Some of the food is faster than he is," I say.

Bear gives up, steps away from the carrousel, tray mounded with meat. He looks around for a while before he spots our table, then starts over with a slow lumber.

I reach for the yams as the corn pudding jerks over, knocking the spoon out of my hand. It sinks into the pinky juice of the yam vat.

"It's kind of tricky, frankly," says Eddie. "At least the salad bar is stationary, the old-fashioned type."

He gestures over toward the short, non-mechanical island, iced vessels of lettuce and tomato wedges, tubs of dressings. The only patrons at the salad bar are two elderly women in matching purple sweat suits.

They stand at one end, staring down the counter with their bowls in their hands, waiting with pious patience for the ham bits and radishes to move their way.

* * *

Bear grins up at us over quantities of bad meat, hands slathered in barbeque sauce to the wrists, sauce dripping from his chin, painted across his cheeks, his lips, a dab on the tip of his nose.

We're letting him risk sitting, and he has his elbows braced on the table, giving a riblet a real sloppy blow job, sucking off the sauce, sawing the reconstituted pork product back and forth across his mouth like a boneless harmonica.

I remember a line of Shivaji McArthur's: "Your other white wormy planks of pressed cartilage."

The cowboy crowd starts chanting: "Pork chops. Pork chops. Pork chops." Bear drops the remaining rind of riblet, picks at the flaky pastry shell of his shepherd's pie.

I remember a holiday with Padhya and Padhya's mother, her father busy somewhere, called away by an emergency page. Gingerbread, pineapple, mint: The stiflingly sweet smell of frosting floating thick across the air.

Padhya was angry, had been crying, sitting with a new best-selling book on blood disease, bundled up by the drained swimming pool, its emptiness masked by a drum-tight blue tarp spotted with dead leaves.

Her mother and I sat across from each other at the kitchen table, our faces hidden from each other by the flowers I ordered for Padhya, a seasonal bouquet, the colors of a fox hunt.

Padhya's mother said something about "the drama of medicine," her voice lilting and bored, the tall glass cabinet behind her back, her collection of porcelain figurines, milkmaids and mandolin players, a dust-free Victorian world, hints of blush-tone color over the folds and smooth bends of glossy, white skin…

Eddie slathers apple butter over a corn stick, and I have to look away. Every honey-sweetened bite of hush puppy tastes vaguely like you.

The black slats of the window blinds are thick with dust. Beyond them, a winged sign towers above this truck stop plaza. Scrolling yellow lights flash the time and temperature, the price of gas and diesel, the sale on AM/FM radios at the Souvenir Shoppe, certified CAT scales, specials on warm pie slices.

I hear myself ask about the plans for Cleveland, and Eddie starts a speech about how after we drop the llama off, he wants to hang out in Coventry for a while, with his sister's ex-boyfriend, the poet and taxidermy artist.

"The kid's *crazy*. He's got a freezer full of dead animals. He collects them, sketches them, poses them, uses them as parts for robots, as furniture."

"Why'd your sister break up with him?"

"I have no idea. But he's still absolutely in love with her. He just sits around his studio, drunk on kosher wine, weaving heart-shaped baskets out of cat gut."

"I kind of thought we were just going to unload the llama, head right back home…"

"Nah, man. I mean, we're going to go all the way up there, might as well kick back, maybe have some drugs, talk about art. He's a really exciting guy, always talking about how 'the materials should be as difficult to work with and experience as the subject matter.' Just talking to him on the phone yesterday really got my head spinning about all kinds of possibilities for the Kent State project. I don't want to sound like Kim or something, but, you know, the potentials of taxidermy modeling, the audience's ability to engage with the imagery of *butchery*…"

Bear's pie ruptures, cubed carrots and pale peas oozing out in a sea of gravy, flooding against the fish nuggets, the collected bones of chicken wings.

He keeps eating, wiping chunks of fried fish across the pool of gravy, lifting them dripping to his lips. The fish breaks apart, dropping back to the tray—scaly, silver slivers coating his fingers with beefy-brown slime. He sucks his fingers clean, licks his palm.

I feel myself stand up, turn, begin to walk away, past the cowboy table, covered in buffet vats, several baskets from the bread line. They've even set up one of the free-standing sneeze guards from the salad bar as a centerpiece.

I walk past them, away from the slow grind of the buffets, past the cash register, the coat racks, to the bank of pay phones by the video arcade, the claw machine, the driving and shooting simulators.

The coins drop into the pay phone's hollow gut, and the dial tone comes, then disappears.

I get her machine, and when I speak, it is as if my voice is already a recording, playing back muffled, metallic, distant, and weak.

* * *

Bear makes it back to the truck on his own, though we have to help him a little when it comes to navigating the climb into the passenger seat.

The food in his belly livens him up enough that he can stay seated without falling asleep.

We don't take the Interstate on, but follow a two-laner back further and further into the country, strips of wispy clouds scouring the sky the color of aluminum.

Eddie's sorting through loose cassettes strewn at his feet. He picks one from under the brake pedal, tosses it behind him, where it hits me on the side of the face. The truck wobbles to the right, dips onto the gravel shoulder. Eddie straightens up and steers again.

"I'm looking for that PSA mix I was telling you about. The archives tape. You've at least got to hear the one that got Tegan into so much trouble."

Bear turns at the mention of her name, makes a noise like he's trying to speak. Then he smiles, starts to hum, some droning, atonal tune which I think may be a slowed-down version of "Lots of Danger (Don't Park Next to Vans at Night)."

"Hey, good to have you back, Bear," says Eddie. "I'll need your muscle here pretty soon. All those horse hormones are going to pay off. How much do you figure a llama weighs, Wheeler? A dead one, I mean. I guess we have to figure that in, too. The dead are heavier than the living."

We pass a billboard for a car dealership on the other side of the state, a billboard with the bee mascot of a defunct fast-food burger chain.

* * *

I remember the thick red shag of her bedroom's carpet, lying there with the stereo on, and MTV, not that I can remember any songs.

She was flipping through catalogues, sighing with each page turned, circling items for relatives in other cities to buy her for her birthday.

I was next to her, sketching from her zoological coloring book, copying out the inner anatomy of pork tape worms, Asian liver flukes, charts of superficial and deep dissections of fetal pigs.

She picked up a remote control, turning down the volume on one of the songs, said something about mitochondria being their own creatures, protozoan living symbiotically within our cells.

Then her cousin called from New York, and she jumped up, paced with the phone, carried it into the closet, described her new shoes, laughed at some joke about the names of grocery stores in Ohio, about me.

That afternoon we drove in a blizzard to the gas station for candy bars, snow swirling in closed currents, a bright gauze over the air, thick, sugary frosting over the slopes of the country club's golf course.

When we stopped, broad flakes burned to tears

against our reddened cheeks, blowing in blinding white gusts against our faces.

Then back to the warmth of her house, toffee bars and the gas fire crackling through its hearth speakers, the cases of china and porcelain figurines, the gurgle as the fountain trickled its loop of water over rocks, everything as domestic as the tiny terra-cotta pots of lemongrass on the sill above the stove, my hands on her hips as she stood at the boiling water tap mixing us mugs of powdered cocoa.

"Not here," she said, and we waited till we were upstairs, locked away, to touch. With the lights out and the curtains drawn, as she pulled her sweater over her turtleneck, static sparked in the dark.

* * *

Eddie takes the cigarette from his mouth, uses it to light his next one as we pass an abandoned general store, its windows boarded up, its sign advertising a discontinued brand of lemon-lime pop.

I say, "Here's something I've been thinking about, every now and again, for a while. In high school, I had this algebra teacher. Mr. Gordon. Like you'd expect, he had a mustache, wore clothes in primary colors, blue slacks, red sports jacket, bad fabric that gave off that wrinkle-free smell when he sweated, which he did profusely, especially by fifth period. He picked his ears when he lectured, doused himself in aftershave to cover the stench of gin. He coached the girls' volleyball team, wore a whistle around his neck."

"Pervert," says Eddie. "Tell me this isn't a story about his daughter. What makes people such fucking bastards, such God damn monsters?"

"But that's not it," I say. "He didn't have a daughter.

He'd been married, divorced, but no children. He was having an affair with Ms. Harris, this business school student who was hired as a part-time typing instructor, like twenty years younger than him. She taught the early morning typing class."

"Typing class. There was time well spent."

"At my school it was required, but didn't fit into the college-prep schedule, so all us kids in that track had to show up to school an hour early, add an extra period to our day, *morning* typing class, an hour of formatting business letters, running speed trials. And there wasn't any correction fluid."

"Why'd we have to go to high school again?" says Eddie. "I think my only decent high school memories revolve around liquid paper. Honest, I feel seriously disadvantaged by the whole high school thing. Four years of my life. Paying those stupid service charges outside liquor stores. All that abrasive, anti-acne facial scrub. And... what's the word... *frontage*?"

Bear burbles contentedly.

At the old, burnt-out shell of a rural church, its charred cross and steeple still standing, we make a turn. There's a little graveyard at its side, stones random as a pumpkin patch, which pretty soon we pass for real, orange orbs vining along the ground.

"Anyway," I say. "One day we had a substitute for Algebra and then a few days later somebody complained to the manager of this hotel outside town, a smell, a problem with flies, and Mr. Gordon was found hanging from the ceiling fan. The details are sketchy, but after they found him Ms. Harris wrecked her car, drunk, drinking as she drove, just racing up and down the Turnpike in her Buick. She cut her face, right like this, straight from one end to the other, this thick scar, all the way to the chin, but she didn't die. She still teaches typing every morning at seven o'clock, though I heard she dropped out of business school. She's still just part-time faculty."

A sign with a black silhouette of a slow child at play and mailboxes clustered at the shoulder in tall stacks like beehives count as a town, sanction a change in speed limit.

We pause at the single four-way stop, two corners of which are vacant lots. Of the other two corners, one is a tavern, the other a gas station/mini-mart. There are posters for snuff in the windows of both establishments, men in hunting gear and face paint in each parking lot.

The men glare at our truck, counting out ammunition, loading their rifles and shotguns. Then, as we pass, one guy sees my cap, raises his beer in salute.

Eddie says, "Here's something I've been thinking about, every now and again, for a while. So there are cinnamon-raisin bagels, right? And there are apple-cinnamon cereals, but why aren't there raisin-cinnamon bagels, cinnamon-apple cereals?"

We're in forest now, trees close to the road, no shoulder. The road curves up in a hairpin, drops down with one of those sudden, stomach-tingling falls.

"I mean," says Eddie, "It's not a matter of ingredient order, is it? Is cinnamon somehow more important in the one and less important in the other? And I don't think it reflects any kind of aesthetic considerations. Consumers would be just as drawn to cinnamon-apple as to apple-cinnamon, right?"

I'm thinking of the plastic scepter in my hand, the spotlight's hot amber against her face, about how we've lived since, somehow placated by that hollow high school fame or, minutes before, the melancholy of a back road, the gravel moaning under the wheels as she pulled to the shoulder, rolled to a slow stop, switching the tape in the deck to the makeout mix, unlatching her bra and pulling it out one of her sleeves so she "wouldn't get poked by the underwire once we start." Me, coming in my briefs, a yellowing crust on the second joint of the finger I pull from her cunt.

A man in a shaggy, moss-colored face mask drags something bloody behind him, out of the woods, toward a pickup parked a ways behind us, in the ditch.

He waves at me, gives me a thumbs up.

"It's alphabetical," I say.

Bear burps with sudden pleasure.

"Ham on rye?" says Eddie. "Cheese omelet? Cucumber dill? Cherry wheat? Bacon, lettuce, and tomato? My God, Wheeler, the whole world, the whole world's set up alphabetically."

Before long, the last of the trees thin out, fields now, a few farmhouses, but spaced far apart. We come to four lone traffic lights rocking on their wires over a crossroads at the corner of four harvested fields, crows gleaning in the husky, battered land.

There's a trio of storage silos in the distance, and near them a long building, a couple of smaller barns. As we get closer, I see that this is the llama farm, a fence by the road, the mud-brown field dotted with clumps of munching wool back by the barns.

But we drive on, passing the gate to the drive, the rest of the fence.

"Hey, Yoder," I say. "Wake up."

"I told you, Wheeler, don't make jokes about sleep. We're going a little bit further, a different place."

* * *

A pack of snarling mutts meet us at the gate of the Nuhauser & Son Christmas Tree Farm. They leap around, snapping at each other and the windows of the truck as we roll up the gravel drive.

Bear seems to be growling in response to them.

One dog lands on the hood, slobbering against the cracked section of the windshield as he tries to bite through. His fangs scrape the glass and Eddie says, "Easy, easy. Bear, he's probably going to break through in a minute. Wheeler, there should be one of those small Army-issue shovels back there, maybe under the passenger seat…"

There's a blast, and the dog jumps off, runs off with the others into the grid of small firs that stretches out beside the road.

A man walks up to Eddie's window and taps the smoking barrel of his big silver handgun against it.

"You Yoder?" the man says.

Eddie rolls down the glass, exchanges some kind of handshake with the guy.

"Third shed on the left, pull right on in there, I'll close it up after you."

The road curves up a slight rise toward the farmhouse, then splits off into a paved lot and a dirt access road running past three outbuildings. A couple of trucks, an old tractor, and a battered station wagon are parked in the lot, a big, freshly-cut fir strapped to the luggage rack of the car with bungee cables.

We turn in at the third outbuilding. The older trees are on this side of the road, the tallest farthest away, aged layers of height, from over eight feet down to about four feet at the roadside.

The outbuilding has a wide wooden barn door in front, open, and Eddie noses the truck inside. The air is heavy with the dusty green smell of pine needles.

Various saws and rope slings hang from the wall, a hopper of some kind, a riding mower. There's another pickup parked inside, too, which we pull alongside.

In its bed, partly covered by some canvas, is the llama—gray, incompletely sheared, head hidden but legs sticking out, fluffy below the knees, like it's wearing fur leggings.

Flies clot around the body. Even inside the sealed cab, I can hear their buzzing.

The building goes dark as the man with the gun closes the door, then a bulb snaps on above us, hanging down on a wire between the two trucks.

The man circles around to Eddie's side, says, "Well, get out. I ain't lifting it again." His gun has been put away somewhere, it seems.

The man wears a corduroy jacket, glasses that are actually goggles, the kind professional athletes sometimes wear.

He says, "We took most of the wool, not that it was in too good a shape. Thing's been dead a while now, was probably dead a full day before I got it back here."

Eddie motions for me to stay in the truck, tells Bear to help him. They climb out. Eddie still has Bear's wallet in his pocket, and he takes it out, hands a few bills to the man.

"This here's a real bargain for you, kid," the man says. "Good thing your boy just wants the bones, though. I figure they'll clean off just fine, but damn that smell until you're rid of the meat."

Eddie swats some flies away from his face. He climbs into the bed of the other truck, pushes the llama out toward Bear, who grabs it by the back legs. Together, they lift it up and drop it down into the bed of Eddie's truck.

"You know, Yoder," the man says, "I've heard about you. You're right, of course, about the whole thing—the angle, the timing, the whole damn confusion over the brain. Lone gunman, my ass."

Eddie nods, shrugs. He's wrapping up the llama in the canvas from the other truck.

The man says, "Figured you'd want that critter covered driving all around Cleveland with it, so I soaked those old burlap bags in insecticide. The last thing you and your boy need is them flies when you start cutting into it."

The dogs are back, outside the door, yelping and snarling, tossing themselves against the wood, scraping at it with their claws.

"Sure as shit got my dogs excited. Dogs and llamas, I don't know what it is between 'em. Hard candy?" The man takes something from his mouth. "Organic. Honey and gingko. Good for the memory."

"No, thanks."

"Suit yourself."

Eddie and Bear get back into the truck, both stinking of the llama, a smell like wet socks and link sausages frying in lard, a smell that reminds me of my grandmother's house.

The man pats the hood of our truck, nods at Eddie. He draws his gun again, walks back around and swings the door open, firing once into the sky.

We back out, turn around on the gravel. The dogs close in quickly, and the man fires two more shots, both at the road, blasting chunks of rock up around the dogs.

They retreat again, one of the smaller dogs snapping at a bigger one's flank on the way. The big dog turns, grabs the other's neck in his jaw, spins back around, flipping him up through the air.

The man fires a final shot, directly overhead, gives us a slow wave as we tear off down the drive, dust rolling up behind us, the gravel gritting and roaring under the tires.

One dog gives chase, but stops at the gate, where we spin hard onto the road, the llama sliding across the bed.

Once we're past the traffic light again I say, "Did we just buy a black market llama, Yoder?"

"Bear bought it," he says. "But Shivaji's reimbursing you and me. Fifty each."

"Oh," I say. "Ok."

* * *

With our cargo bundled in insecticide-drenched burlap back in the bed, we make quick time to the Interstate, where the measured cadence of speed slips Bear back into deep sleep.

Fall's most blunted stages face us along the roadside, trees yellowed out like old photographs, trees still clinging to mute greens, patches of brown, and some, the eager and the weak, already bare.

There are no bright colors here, where the seasons come and go like business days, like freight. We are driving into a literal place, where all flames are saved for fire.

Is there anything more anguished than a straight, streaking track of highway, grooved like an old wound with that ditch in between?

This feeling of far away, the landmarkless expanse, the same shiny silver-green signs, with only the names and numbers changing as we move through time and space.

The road ahead, and ahead, and closer to something now, an outskirt-village water tower, mushroom-bulbed, at the next rise. Snow fences, the swift, dense press of speed.

Evergreens planted against the ever gray, a growing thickness at the sides of the road as the hotels begin, and cars line up and wait to merge from the ramps.

* * *

Bear's parents live in a fabricated colony at the southern end of Cleveland's urban sprawl, a subdivision of winding roads named in honor of non-indigenous plants.

The houses, spaced between flat, golf-green lawns, arranged around an intricate maze of circular cul-de-sacs, offer variations on a basic architectural model. There's the house with one gable, garage at left, in pink, the house with one gable, garage at right, in beige. There's the house with two gables, garage at left, in yellow, and etc., etc., etc., with picket fences in sections, fulfilling no real fence function, just a decorative aspect, a few yards' worth running parallel to a sidewalk or a house's front.

We pass several houses with seasonal displays, small hay bales stacked on porches, accentuated with dried corn stalks and, in one case, a scarecrow.

Bear's parents' house sits at the dead end of Cottonwood, two gables, garage at the right, white with pink trim. A large grapevine wreath hangs from the front door, and the mailbox at the curb has a painting of a kitten and a puppy curled together on a blue pillow.

"Dr. Carlyle and Dr. Carlyle," reads the sign atop the mailbox.

Bear wakes with a grunt. He coughs, swallows, reaches for his mouth as he lets out a short, liquid belch, then swallows again. His skin is pale and runny, the hair on the back of his neck matted down with sweat.

Eddie says something about holding it, and we park at the next hydrant.

I climb out after Eddie and help Bear out of the cab. He drops to his knees as soon as he's on the ground, groaning, holding his gut.

"Ah, come on," says Eddie. "No complications. We're almost *there*."

We lift him up, me under one arm, Eddie under the other, walk him up the street to the driveway. He's shivering, his lips tinted with a touch of blue. He gags, burps, swallows heavily. As we pass the mailbox, he lets out a long moan.

"Alright," says Eddie. "New plan. We prop him here, ring the doorbell, and run."

"He's sick," I say. "We should at least get him inside."

Bear pulls away from us, takes a step back, gasping. He turns toward the lawn and vomits in one single, solid, arching stream.

Eddie jumps to the porch, hits the doorbell button.

Bear's vomit, which is thick, freshly-chewed, with recognizable clots of riblet matter and a small candied-apple ring, begins to flow down the driveway toward the gutter.

He burps again, coughs. He works his tongue around in his cheeks, then spits a fatty wad of partially digested homestyle cooking down the driveway.

Someone inside the house laughs, a shrill sound, more like a scream. Bear spits again, wipes his mouth with the back of his hand.

Eddie and I are asking him if he's in good enough shape to walk when the door opens, a man in shorts, the first two fingers of his right hand buried in his mouth up to the knuckles. He laughs, says, "Junior," and pulls his fingers free with a hard suck and pop, sloshing pink liquid from the martini glass in his left hand, soaking part of a green paper umbrella and knocking off some kind of plastic animal. "Well, well, well," he says. "If this isn't *quite* the surprise."

He takes a quick, slurped drink as he wipes his other hand against his Hawaiian-print shirt and his-madras print Bermuda shorts and extends it toward me.

"Hello to you two, too. Warren Carlyle, Senior, but that's bound to get confusing, and anyway, everyone calls me Errol." He winks. "Unless they're being *rude*."

"Then what do they call you?" says a voice from further inside the house. A pair of fat, long-haired cats rub against his bare, hairy legs, until the larger of the two looks up at Bear and immediately arches its back, hissing.

I slip my hand inside my pocket, wiping it off on the lining. Errol shakes hands with Eddie, says, "Don't mind the hands, boys, just a bit of an accident with the cocktail olives," then yells over his shoulder, "Marilyn? Marilyn, it's Warren. And these other boys."

There's a woman's yelp, then a female voice says, "We better get decent then, and quick."

Laughter and applause from the back room scares out a few more cats, one of which, a scrawny Siamese, does a mid-air turn when it spots Bear, bolting up the staircase behind Errol.

"Well, come on in, out of the cold. We're taking a stand against this horrific shift in weather. Back in the living room, it's summer in California."

He leads us into the house, down a hallway lined with paintings of game, a pair of pronghorn at sunset, a cougar and her cubs, several of ducks and quail and pheasants.

"The Rosemonts are here, a few cocktails, a few friendly wagers on the Rumicub, soaking up a few gigawatts of halogen-supplement sunbeams. Might want to peel those jackets back, boys."

A woman tiptoes toward us wearing a strapless summer dress, shoeless, her stockings dangling a few inches at the toes. She drops her jaw in mock surprise.

"Oh, it *is* Warren. Lenny, Peg, you remember our son Warren? And these must be some of his friends. Well, well, it is *always* good to meet friends of Warren."

Bear stares straight ahead, his eyes glossed over. Drool builds at the side of his mouth.

Marilyn winks at Errol, mouths a phrase I can't make out, her lips thick with deep red lipstick, smeared rough at the corners.

Errol's shirt hangs open well below the beginnings of chest hair so ample it looks like a solid pad of salt-and-pepper steel wool. He smiles and holds his wife by the waist.

We follow them back to the living room, several dark strands of hair sprouting up over Errol's collar, Marilyn swishing her skirt hem, running through some dance steps, shoulders twitching.

Bear goes limp, slides down, Eddie bracing him for a second before I can get under his other arm again. We drag him the rest of the way.

A floor-to-ceiling bay window dominates the living room, looking out on the subdivision's woods, a turpentine sky. Arranged in front of the window are three tall banks of halogen lights, blasting the room with white heat, glaring off the coffee table and the semi-circle of reclining plastic beach chairs.

Peg Rosemont stretches out in one of these, wearing sunglasses, a bikini top, and a pair of rolled-up denim shorts. She stares over the rim of her glasses, fans herself with a copy of some glossy celebrity magazine with the word "Divorce" in its headline.

"Hello, company," she says. "We're pretending it's summer."

Lenny Rosemont makes a practice swing, then knocks a putt across the carpet. He wears a pair of Speedos and a scuba mask tilted back over his forehead, blue zinc streaked over his nose.

He salutes us with his fat plastic golf club as the mechanical alligator into which he knocked the ball swallows, spins around, and fires the ball back in his direction.

Another pair of cats rub at Peg's feet. Four or so are curled together on the sofa. One particularly fluffy foreign-looking type hunches under the coffee table, stalking the alligator.

Bear groans, his mouth hanging open. He breathes in a struggled way, half pant, half dry heave. Eddie and I prop him against the mantelpiece, where a calico licks at a bowl of potpourri.

"Errol, does this boy look like he's feeling alright?" says Marilyn.

She presses the back of her hand against her son's forehead, then passes her drink to Eddie so she can hold Bear's face in both of her hands. She has a quarter-size blue bruise on her neck.

"His skin is as pale as— Oh, Errol, feel this boy, he's absolutely soaked through."

Eddie says, "He's kind of fatigued. That's actually why we brought him up here. I think he needs a few days of good, solid rest."

"Well, Errol, he's clammy, and his pulse... He needs to get right into bed. Fatigue, I guess. I told you about that school, competition all the time."

"Junior, you heard your mother. Double time, up to bed."

Eddie guides him by his shoulders, points him back toward the door, the stairwell. Bear stumbles back, steadies.

"Maybe somebody should give him a hand?" I say.

Eddie's still holding Marilyn's drink, which she stirs with a finger. She tucks a piece of his hair back into his sock cap, coos, sucks on the stirring finger as she studies his face.

Errol has a silver shaker, mixing the next round.

Peg says "You're ten minutes too late, company. If you'd been here ten minutes ago, you could have tried my fantastic crab balls."

"We had a big lunch," says Eddie, attempting to offer Marilyn her drink again. She doesn't take it, so he puts in on the mantle, where it is immediately lapped at by the mantle cat.

"Those crab balls absolutely disappeared. It was like one those things on television, all the starving refugees, those air-dropped bags of dried rice."

Bear crumples against the wall by the stairwell, skewing the photo of mountain goats but not knocking it down. One hand splayed against the wall, he lifts himself back up and continues.

Lenny knocks a hollow, plastic golf ball against my sneaker. "My wife thinks the worst thing about being in a displaced persons' camp would be the food," he says.

"Starch, starch, starch," says Peg.

Errol grabs my shoulder with a wet hand. "Don't get too close to the halogens," he says. "Last Thanksgiving some old biddy set her ermine stole on fire."

"That would have been my *mother*, you cur," says Marilyn.

* * *

My breath wheezes, a corridor tightening between my lungs and my throat. My eyes water at the edges. I keep blinking, letting tears run down my cheeks.

A shallow porcelain bowl full of water sits on the coffee table, a large, open rose petal and a thick scum of cat hairs floating in it.

"Say, Wheeler," says Eddie. "Aren't you allergic to—"

Errol slaps us both on the back. "So," he says. "How

is life at the big school? Not studying all the time, I hope. Those Marxist profs sure ran our son ragged."

Lenny reaches out with his kiddie golf club and lifts up the back of Marilyn's skirt. She spills part of her new drink on the carpet, and Lenny starts laughing, snorting, pounding the floor with his club.

"Don't mind us," says Peg. "We're all just a touch *perverse*."

"Just a touch," says Lenny.

"I miss that little school," says Marilyn. "Errol and I just can't visit enough. You'd love it, Peg, so quaint, pathways and buildings. Amish."

"An Amish University?" says Lenny.

"An Amish area."

"Amish *territory*," says Errol. "That's the correct jargon, isn't it, boys?"

"Aren't you going to offer company a cocktail, Errol?" says Peg.

Marilyn says, "He can't say he's forgetting his manners, because he never had any. He's just casual trash, boys, doesn't have a bloodline to support him."

Lenny putts a series of balls at a sleeping cat, two of them smacking against the animal before it runs away, one more catching it as it goes.

"Shoo, kittens, go," says Marilyn. "Sometimes they spit up on strangers."

"Really, boys," says Errol. "I'm goddamn sorry. Do you want a little drink? For the road?"

"Oh, for Christ's sake," says Lenny. "They're Amish, man."

"They're not Amish. The school—"

Marilyn says, "I do hope everything's still good between Warren and Laura. I always have liked that Laura, though we haven't seen her since, when was it, dear, last Thanksgiving?"

"Were we here last Thanksgiving?"

"Warren came up, and Laura. She helped me make my fabulous yam casserole. Oh, but we saw her in December, too, when we went down to visit the campus. You remember December, honey? We met Laura's roommate, that filthy little dancer?"

"Let's drink to our new friends," says Lenny. "I don't know any Amish toasts, but you look like good, high quality people to me."

Every inch of my skin surface itches. Sacks below my eyes are inflating, billowing up like twin air bags. I'm doing candle-blowing exercises, my breath like a rusty hinge.

Eddie says, "You don't look so good or high quality, man."

"Could be the Asian flu," says Errol. "It's that time of year again, and the dreaded disease is predicted to be stronger than ever this season."

Marilyn says, "Give them some samples, dear."

Errol steps across to a roll-top desk, slides up the top, sorts through a series of pigeon holes, a collection of small boxes. He stands and moves with his elbows bent at ninety-degree angles, his hands dangling as if they'd just been sterilized and he's about to reach for a doggie scalpel, a pair of kitty tongs. He finds what he's looking for, locks the desk top, and comes back to Eddie with a square box slashed in a bright pattern of green and blue.

"These'll give your immune systems a boost. Still marketed for dairy cattle, but our body chemistry is far more similar than you'd imagine."

I say, "I think it's just allergies, really."

"Well, we've got some things for that, too. Mix caution with preparedness, as they say. I get all these from the pharmaceutical companies. A growing new field, animal drugs."

Eddie nods with vehemence, takes the box of cow pills. "There *is* something nasty going around," he says.

I step around the halogen banks and stand in front of the window, the brown woods looking as if the season came on with chemical defoliants.

Dry, dead branches splay out under the overcast sky, a metal No Hunting sign nailed to one of the closer, larger trunks, dented in silver flecks from buck shot.

Marilyn comes up beside me, stirring a new drink with the toothpick handle of a paper umbrella.

She says, "The woods are lovely this time of year, but we do have a problem with hunters. They just come too close. We've lost more than a few cats since we moved here."

Lenny says, "These Amish boys look a little like hunters to me."

"The hat was a gift," I say. "Eddie's a vegetarian."

Errol slaps his palm against his forehead.

"You crazy kids with your *alternative* lifestyles. In that case, you better take a least two of these a day if you plan on functioning at all on that anemic, low-protein, *nonsense* diet."

He goes back to the desk, comes out with three flat boxes, yellow and brown. He hands them to Eddie, who nods with the gravity of the ill.

"God," says Peg. "I was wondering what happened to the poor boy's *fingernails*."

"This one's put out for big game," says Errol. "Predators, carnivores. Give you the strength of ten tigers."

"Do you have anything for cysts?" says Eddie. He holds up his wrist, bends it down, the bony orange knob sticking up like an extra thumb.

Lenny says, "Have you tried the magnet therapy? Remarkable. Very low incidence of cysts among the Orientals. I know. I served over there."

Peg drops her magazine, covers her ears with her hands. "No more war stories."

Lenny takes a swing toward the mouth of the alligator. "Good *work ethic* is what you people have," he says. "I don't agree with that *taboo* against electronic equipment, but piety, honesty, hard labor: We need more of that in this country. I'd certainly consider the benefits of a strong, disciplined Amish education. If Peg and I were lucky enough to have a child…"

"I said *no war stories*."

Eddie's at the rolltop desk, testing the lock.

A framed photograph hangs above the desk, a whale breeching, its weight suspended in a frozen heave. A great arc of froth trails behind, a constellation of liquid beads. The inevitable crash of mass back into the black water suspended, the beast lingers, silent, in space and time.

"That was taken out in California," says Errol. "The Pacific Coast. We just moved here three years ago, the year before Warren went off to school. We're still very much Californians at heart."

"Do you work much with the large marine mammals?" I say.

Everyone laughs.

"No, no," says Marilyn. "We only treat *real* animals. *Domesticated*. Kittens, puppies, household pets."

Her hand is on my back, pressing me gently but clearly toward the door. Errol walks along beside Eddie, saying something about his own college years.

"Do visit again," says Marilyn.

She is holding my hand by the fingers, shaking it the way one shakes hands with a dog. We are standing at the base of the stairwell, and Errol opens the front door.

"So long," he says.

Peg hasn't moved from her beach chair, but Lenny

stands in the door of the living room, giving us a formal military salute with his plastic putter.

"*Auf Wiedersehen,*" he says.

* * *

The blacktop road twists out of this soft-toned, vinyl-sided subdivision. Eddie makes another wrong turn, swings the truck around in the dead end.

I'm in the front seat, face pressing against the window, cap brim folded down over my face. Eddie rolls his window down, turns the air conditioning on, fans full force.

"Sorry that window doesn't roll down, man. Can you breathe at all? Just, like, give me some kind of sign if you stop breathing, ok?"

"I'll pass out, how about that?"

"That's good. I think I've got some gum, and there's bottled water in back, in the duffel bag. No, no, no, what am I thinking? *Ephedrine*, that'll clear you right up."

He's rummaging through the glove compartment, tossing out empty cigarette packs, wadded maps, parking tickets, an unrolled condom.

The truck jumps the curb at the next bend in the road, rumbles across the edge of a lawn, clattering through a lone segment of picket fencing.

Eddie sits up, pulls the truck back on course, his right hand still tossing out used Kleenex and cassette cases from the glove compartment.

"Bingo," he says.

He holds up a withered, red paper pouch, hands it to me.

"Are there any left?"

I unfold the top, where it's been ripped open, and shake out three white pills, scored across the top into four pie-shaped sections.

"Three," I say.

"Take two," he says. "And one for me."

He dry-swallows his pill, beats a new pack of cigarettes against his thigh, rips off the cellophane cover with his teeth.

A final white fence plank dislodges from the bumper, flipping out and slapping against the sidewalk.

"Bracing pep," he says. "You think Bear's dead yet?"

I say, "His parents might not notice."

* * *

The first people of Ohio were mound builders, immovable in the belief that nothing is as powerful as a lump on the horizon. They stacked rock and earth atop their corpses, raising monuments to the land from the land itself. With tools of sharpened stone, jewels dredged from the rivers, these people paid solemn homage to the seasons, the endless cycle of life and death, the grist mill of the sun. Ages of blood-drenched history have brought us here, a rotating plastic moon above an outdoor equipment outlet.

Eddie shifts lanes, maneuvers around a rust-riddled dump truck, shovel wedged between metal straps on its side. The traffic splits, and we loop up, matching velocity with elevation, rising above spoiled fields, mud cross-hatched with pipelines and conveyor belts, slag heaps and coal piles, tarps held down with chains and cinder blocks.

Stacks belch blue and orange flames, fire dissolving into black, greasy smoke, smoke that stumbles out, drags itself like a gutter-bound drunk across the sky.

Eddie scans through the stations for an appropriate tune.

Cleveland is ringed in concentric circles, zones of impact, the malignant industrial wasteland surrounding the older, coal dust-coated realm of flat warehouse roofs, disjointed Orthodox crosses competing with billboards for malt liquor and unfiltered cigarettes, all empty space boarded up, rooftops crusted with sparkling, late-night broken-bottle glass, flowering graffiti and gang tags, police line snapping like streamers, spray-paint squiggles on the side of a car, tires stripped, propped on cement blocks at the roadside, orange tickets stuck across its windshield, flapping.

We sink straight into Cleveland's excrescent heart, a soul of flat-rate parking structures, the clock-like echo of hollow pavement. The downtown towers stand like ambushed soldiers, like taller, weaker versions of the grim bridge guardians standing watch in stone, all swords and shoulders and square-cut wings.

As Eddie hovers over an FM station, someone dies on the traffic report.

The radio voice paces professionally over the script, breaking the bad news to the south-bound commuters: "One lane, almost at a stand-still, gaper's delay west-bound, equipment on the scene."

On a road bleached white by the salt of endless winters, I taste your skin again, and think of its every fold and curve, the soft top of your hand, your earlobe's flap, your nicotine-drenched hair, all the rich broths and oils and butters inside.

I think of you as heat and proximity and need, your body boundless in its ability to respond, squirming to press closer, hands and mouth searching, reacting, a constant hunger for a deeper push. I don't know if I love Padhya anymore or not, but I am hard just from thinking about you.

The DJ segues back into a song, some dumb screaming,

this newly established outsider sound, a gentle thrashing commodity, an accessible, polite, and polished rage.

Under the ebony speakers of the entertainment center, Padhya and I picnicked on the coffee table, canned delicacies scavenged from the walk-in larder lined with bottles of marinade, thick with the stuffy smell of mail-order spice sets. We ate boxed breadsticks, olives, vegetarian paté. There was a miniature crock of soft cheese, a jar of old caviar. We listened to some TV talk show she didn't want to miss, a television interview with a rock star who lost his legs in a bombing, who bred show dogs somewhere in the Black Forest. Then the talk shifted to prosthesis, to artificial electronic nerves, and Padhya wasn't really eating, anyway, just lifting something to her lips sometimes, in a pause on the television, smearing caviar or paté across her plate with a brittle, dusty rod of bread.

I stared out at the tree stumps by the new pool, the little gods lined along the bookshelf of medical melodrama and true tales of survival, the memoirs of sailors and castaways.

The truck turns, and we are in the city, crowds at the bus stops, choking trees, trunks bound in gauze.

And are you buckling against him now, your hair hanging back, strands clinging against the sweat of your neck as he rides you, breath heavy, holding you down?

The splintery expanse opens wider as we drive down Euclid Avenue, buildings burnt out and busted, the blacktop scabs of vacant lots.

The wind plasters trash wrappers against transformer-heavy utility poles, the poles straining up like spires under the city's low-slung ceiling of clouds, this bleak and suffocating sky.

***

As if in response to this slate gray, Cleveland quality of light, the Cafe Tout a l'Heure has no windows.

Silky, sea-green curtains hang in sets along the walls, strung on brass rods, pouting lips of windowsills underneath. But the curtains open to nothing. Instead of windows, there's just more brick wall, fabric parting on masonry, illuminated by spot lights on tracks running along the ceiling, gelled bulbs pooling the artificial light in colors, a blue cast to one wall, a red streak behind the counter, a patch of green floor, yellow, orange.

Padhya waits for me in the light of the sole white bulb, sitting with a textbook at a table for two beneath a fake window in the far corner of the Cafe Tout a l'Heure.

She has the look of a woman engrossed in reciting, from memory, the names of the major arteries of the human body.

Her dress is a floral print, black, slashed with silver and brown. She chews a thumbnail as she reads, her hand held bent at the wrist, veins out, tenderness exposed.

My familiarity with her body both drains and substitutes for sexual appeal, her sloping shelf of breasts, how her thin neck angles out from the slump of her shoulders.

When I touch her, she starts, looks up, surprised.

"Oh, you're here. Thank God. I was so worried, I was beginning to think— Oh, your *eyes*. Something *did* happen."

She pulls me down into the free chair, nearly knocking her textbook from the tiny tabletop. She extracts a sterilized towelette from her purse, dabs at my eyes with an ethyl-alcohol corner.

"Ow," I say.

"So puffy," she says. "Some discoloration."

"The swelling's going down, actually. I'm fine. Really. It was just... There were just all these cats everywhere."

"Where *were* you? I've been waiting so long, I started imagining things."

"But this is when we were supposed to meet," I say. "I mean, I said four on the phone. It's not even four yet."

"The message said three, but you're here now. And you're ok? I was imagining awful things."

"I'm fine. Just some cats. You?"

"Me? Fine. Good to see you."

She's still examining my eyes. I take her hand, hold it against my cheek.

"Yeah," I say. "Good to see you, too."

I lean over for a kiss, and she twists in for the best fit, a quick, rehearsed connection. She smells of apples and ointment, pulls back as our lips touch, tightens her brow in what I think is facetious annoyance.

"I was supposed to be tutoring someone right now," she says. "You know, that job I have? But whatever, it's good to see you. It was going to be that deaf kid, anyway. I don't know why they assign him to me. He's smart and all, but... You know..."

"He can't hear?" I say.

"That's absolutely the *ugliest* hat."

"I made it in Fabric class," I say.

"I hope you failed," she says, pushing it back farther on my head. "So what brings you up here, anyway? I know you didn't come all the way to Cleveland just to visit your girlfriend."

"Um, Eddie and I, we had to drive up that guy Bear, the big one, wears all the lumberjack flannel..."

"I remember. He has that bitch of a girlfriend, doesn't wash her hair, looks like she has an eating disorder."

"She's a dancer."

"That's a reason, not an excuse." She touches the top of her hair, her ponytail pulled back tight, hair flush against her skull, a solid sheen of hair spray cut with comb marks.

"Anyway," I say. "Bear was feeling kind of sick. Well, he did some bad drugs, some walrus darts, something. I don't really know."

"And you brought him all the way up here to the hospital?"

"Yeah," I say. "We did an intervention, checked him into rehab at Metro Health. I mean, it was hard, but for the best. Responsibility and all."

"Convenient that I live up here, too," she says. A hand claws around my thigh. "You've always got a warm place to spend the night."

"We have to get back tonight, actually. I told you that on the phone, too."

"You told the machine, Martin. You haven't told *me* anything yet. I know the difference."

"Look, I'm sorry about the short notice. I just figured—"

"No, no, it's good to see you. I miss you, I'm not saying that. You got my message from Eddie? I tried to call twice after that, actually, but your machine never picked up."

"We've had some problems with our machine," I say.

"Oh, God, Martin, your eyes are really in bad shape. What was it again, silly? There were cats at the hospital?"

"They were on leashes," I say. "In the waiting room. Pet therapy?"

"It would be great if you could stay the night."

"I really can't, Padhya. We have to get back."

"I just thought, I mean, it's so late in the day now. We're hardly going to get to see each other. And where is Eddie, anyway? He must not like me very much."

"I thought maybe you'd like for us to be alone. And anyway, one of his sister's ex-boyfriends lives up here. They're doing taxidermy or something."

"Whatever. It's just that I got a ride over here, so we're going to have to walk back to the dorm. If you're even staying that long."

Our tracts of dialogue are like this hard metal extra-tall stool, where I perch, my knees hitting the table's edge, my seat angled in a slippery slope, the slats of the back curved in to pinch both of my kidneys.

Padhya runs her hand along the side of her head, checking the flatness, making sure everything is frozen properly in place.

She checks her watch, then bites her thumbnail again, staring off at the curtains of the fake windows along the other wall.

"Padhya. Relax, huh? I came to visit *you*."

"I hate it when people tell me to relax, Martin. And you came to drop one of your druggie friends at the rehabilitation clinic."

"Not a *friend*, exactly."

"I'm confused about things, Martin. I'm confused about us. So if it seems like I'm in a bad mood, or like I'm overly distracted, something on my mind, well, it's just that."

"We're the same as we've always been, Padhya."

"Yeah, but we're also not. Right?" She checks her watch again, holds it against her ear, shakes her wrist.

"Has it stopped?" I say.

"What? No, it's working. Sorry."

"Do you have some place you need to be?"

"Tutoring," she says. "But I canceled."

"Ok," I say, my word drowned by a sudden grinding behind the counter, then the rattle and pressure-hiss of steam from the espresso machine. I glance over at the shiny silver shaking works, reminiscent of childhood movie memories, castaways in outer space, the empty cold that silences screams.

Padhya sighs. "Well," she says. "So." A pause. "Should we get some coffee?"

"It does seem to be the trend here."

She smiles, slips a sleeping puppy bookmark into the textbook and folds it shut. The cover is a photo-collage, a huge hypodermic ejecting a rainbow of thin scenes, a doctor pressing a stethoscope to a patient's naked back, a lab worker marking the sides of a flask, a pack of white blood cells surrounding a spiny purple infection. *Adventures in Immunology.*

"I thought they were going to come over and ask me to leave," she says. "I've been here for hours and haven't made a purchase."

"Hours?"

"I hoped maybe you'd be early, and I was expecting you to be on time. But whatever, I needed to get away from Allie, and I've been reading the most fascinating thing."

"Adventures in Immunology?"

She reopens the book, flips back a few pages to a large multi-colored chart, fluctuating lines weaving and sawing across a numerical grid.

"This," she says. "This is a baby born with AIDS."

"Oh," I say. "I wouldn't have known."

"Of course not. Science is about the things we can't see. Direct experience of the progress of disease is rare, so we rely on manufactured graphic representations."

"Is it a he or a she?" I say

She points to some small print at the bottom of the chart. She says, "The subject is male, age three and a half."

"More of a toddler than a baby," I say.

"For the immunologist, the primary data for investigation becomes *data* itself. This is very much a non-interventionist approach."

"All these sharp points, this steady decline, this is something bad, right?"

"You're missing the point. This isn't the way a general practitioner would approach a disease, obviously, but, whatever, immunology isn't primary care, you know?"

She has that old high school giddiness again, that bounce and rapt tone to her voice. She gestures with her hands, tracing half arcs in the air. Her eyes are wide, smiling. The joy of science.

When she first moved to town, before I even knew her, there were a couple of weeks when she attended my college-prep Chemistry class, before they found a way to rearrange her schedule so she could take the advanced-placement version.

The class met mornings, second periods, always charts of coded letters and numbers, snap-together 3-D structures, labs with burners and tubes, all of us in plastic aprons and greasy safety goggles, Padhya in her element, always three steps ahead.

We memorized the charges of ionic compounds and tried to change the color of smoke.

One day we were doing something with petri dishes, sterilization, and Padhya finished so quickly she got to do the whole experiment again, and my lab partner told me to test the tongs against my hand, to tell if they were hot enough, and I burned an "L" into the flesh webbing between my left thumb and forefinger, a sizzle cauterizing away the fast trace of pain.

The wound infected, wet with puss, a slime I scraped out till it finally scabbed and scarred. My lab partner and I got a good laugh out of that, all year.

"Immunologists are concerned with unmediated information," she's saying, "And that kind of objectivity can only be obtained by machines."

I stare back down at the color-coded square, the overlapping strands so close they blur, their subtle shades of variation, almost 3-D, psychedelic.

"That kid born with AIDS is really something," I say.

"Beautiful, isn't it?"

"So," I say. "Coffee?"

* * *

Thermoses of cream, skim, and soy milk sit in a row on the counter above the bowl of sugar cubes, the shakers of vanilla, nutmeg, and cocoa, a plastic bottle of organically processed honey with royal jelly and Echinacea that is *not* shaped like a bear.

A stack of wooden packing crates to the side of the counter displays the Cafe Tout a l'Heure merchandise, the waxed bags of coffee beans, the metal presses, stained-glass jars of hard candy, t-shirts and mugs with reproductions of details from popular impressionist masterpieces and the ubiquitous Cafe Tout a l'Heure logo.

The tanks, spigots, and brewing machines are behind the cash registers, on the other side of the tall glass cabinets of cheesecakes, croissants, individual-size quiches, biscotti biscuits.

I stand on the other side of the register and say, "I'd like a cup of coffee."

The girl in the Cafe Tout a l'Heure apron blows a bit of hair out of her eyes.

"Ethiopian, Kenya AAA, Amazon Blend, or Special Roasted French Vanilla?" she says.

"Just a regular for me."

"Ethiopian, Kenya AAA, Amazon Blend, Special

Roasted French Vanilla: Those are today's coffees, sir. We don't have a *regular*."

"House blend?"

"We have Ethiopian, Kenya AAA, Amazon Blend, and Special Roasted French Vanilla. Which would you like, sir?"

"No, like, generic, just plain coffee?"

"Please, sir, people are waiting. Those are our coffee selections."

"Could you maybe just pick one for me? I mean, sounds like a lot of geography and politics involved. I trust your judgment."

The coffee girl shakes her head, blows another bit of hair out of her eyes. "I'm not allowed to do that, sir. Should I get the manager?"

"Two Ethiopians," says Padhya. "And one cranberry-hazelnut scone."

* * *

I scoop up a handful of sugar cubes and carry them back to our table. Padhya stops to mix some skim milk into her coffee, comes back smiling, her Ethiopian white.

She gives me another bird-like peck on the cheek. "Oh, silly boy. Always putting on a show."

On the walls, between the fake windows, are gilt-frame photographs offering a simplified narrative of coffee production, from the smiling native harvester sweating under his basket of beans to a forklift rolling out crates, culminating with a photo of a man in an office overlooking the Eiffel Tower, sinking a silver spoon into his creamy, rich cup.

"I wasn't putting on a show," I say. "It's just, I mean, you have to be some kind of coffee importer to order at this place."

"So they only have gourmet coffee. That's a good thing. Civilization."

"Ethiopian, Brazil A+, Exotic Coptic Grilled Vinegar Blend. I mean, she was a little bit *wooden* with me, huh?"

"It's the hat, baby. People think you're homeless. But whatever, I love this place. This is what all coffee shops should be like. Have some scone."

She pushes her plate toward me, ceramic scraping across the marble chess board. She nudges the sunken, shriveled, red-specked, butter-crusted pastry lump.

"Yummy," she says.

"I'll pass, thanks. Big lunch."

"Not at the hospital cafeteria, I hope. That filthy hospital. Did I ever tell you that story about the roaches? From my internship there last summer? The oncology ward?"

"Yeah," I say. "I heard the story about the roaches."

"*Public health.* What can you do?"

The table is barely large enough for the inlaid marble tiles to form a complete chess board across the top. Our coffees rest on cardboard coasters shaped like coffee beans, printed with a variety of miniature flags across their surfaces, Cafe Tout a l'Heure, the Tastes of the World.

I lift my cup. The cardboard coffee bean clings to the bottom. There is a warning on the heat sleeve: "Hazardous. Risk of Serious Burns."

She is saying something about the public's lack of concern for themselves, their health and safety. She is quoting her mother: "Dealing with data is so much *cleaner* than dealing with people."

My first sip scalds across my palate, over the top of my tongue. I stifle a hard cough and swallow, heat kicking down my throat, flames expanding inside my chest.

The coaster drops free, slaps against the table top. I put the cup back down on top of it, place a sugar cube inside my mouth, wedge it between my molars and suck.

"So, seriously," she says. "How have you been? I haven't talked to you in months."

"It's just been a couple of days, Padhya."

"Not since we *really* talked. You know what I mean. It's been a long time. I don't even know what to ask. How are classes?"

"Classes are good," I say. "I'm working a lot. I'm told there's a definite expression of feeling in my new pieces, good work with the balance of the scene. How are yours?"

"Alright. Kind of boring, actually. And I'll have the second half of all the boring ones next semester. I should be able to get into some cool classes next year, though."

"I wouldn't want to take classes I didn't like," I say.

"I don't have a choice. It's the program. There's so much general preparatory work that just doesn't excite me, the basis of larger systems, whatever."

She opens her book again, runs her finger down the sharply declining blue slope on the Technicolor chart of the toddler with AIDS.

"I won't be able to take this class till I'm a senior, probably not till grad school unless I get a really high lottery number at registration."

"Lots of numbers," I say.

"It's the purest form of medical science."

I bite into the sugar cube, let its crystals rasp across my raw tongue, sense of taste stripped bare. Only the faintest hint of sweetness remains.

"So, yeah," she says. "My program sucks, but at least it's easy. I have lots of time to tutor, talk on the phone…"

"How's tutoring?"

"Oh, I don't know. I'm making some money, I guess."

She sighs, picks a swollen cranberry from the side of her scone. "Tutoring sucks, too, really."

The scone caves in a bit more, the middle empty, moist and doughy. "At least it will look good on my grad school applications," she says. "You know how it is. We all have to endure things we don't exactly enjoy."

"That's what they say."

"Who?"

"I mean, just the general 'they.' You know, conventional wisdom."

"Hmmm," she says. "Your eyes are getting better, at least. Silly boy, you and your allergies. I read this great article the other day: Reactions, rashes, hives."

"How are you and Allie getting along?" I say. "Didn't you say something on the phone about her?"

"I left a message last week about it. On your machine. It's reassuring to know that you at least listen to your messages, even if you don't call me back."

"You two are still fighting?"

"Yeah, well, kind of. Things would be fine if she weren't just such a bitch."

She moves her finger across her plate, pressing down on all the scone crumbs, collecting them on her fingertip, then wiping them off onto a paper napkin.

* * *

This is what we talk about when we talk about the cliché: My hand seemingly self-impelled in its arc across the tabletop toward her cheek.

She looks up from under her lashes, the dark skin above her eyes. She twists the corners of her mouth, and I say, "I love you, you know?"

We retreat, in response to crises, back to familiar, vacant phrases. A narcotic repetition, a numbed freefall.

"Silly boy," she says.

I lean toward her, and she must move some toward me, too. Our lips meet, press, open in unison. I feel one of my hands slide to her breast, over her heart. She pulls back, holds my wrist.

She says, "Is Eddie just going to pick you up at my dorm?"

"I gave him the number. He said he'd call. He'll need directions."

"I don't know if Allie will be home or not."

"That's alright," I say.

She checks her watch again. "I need to stop at a store," she says. "So drink up."

"I love you," I say, again.

"I know," she says. "But we don't have much time. Let's hurry, ok?"

* * *

Stepping outside is a shock, the world of natural light, the sun beginning to set over Coventry, the air colder than before, a sharp wind of city corners.

The suburban kids who carpool in to play punk for the day are sharing cigarettes and kicking hackey sacks around the concrete shell of the fountain, already dry.

A junior high beggar in new athletic shoes drops to his knees before Padhya.

"Princess, please, spare a quarter? It's my birthday, at least give me a smile."

She steps around him, squeezes my hand.

"Happiness is free," he says.

One of his friends pelts him in the back of the head with a hackey sack.

"I hate this part," says Padhya. "They shouldn't

let these people loiter around here. This is a business district."

We head left at the corner, past the mud-glutted trenches and subterranean chambers of the future parking garage. A chain-link fence shakes on its posts with a cold, dry jangle. Rusty iron reinforcement rods jut from the tops of the concrete pillars.

Hand in hand, Padhya and I walk down the store-lined street, windows crammed with retro and vintage and kitsch, novelty and new age, tie-dyed and rainforest-friendly, Celtic, Indian, homespun, hemp, tribal, and alpaca-wool-blend.

The sun sets without a show, just a descent into darkness, a brightening of the streetlights and shop windows. Padhya rummages through her purse.

"Don't tell me I didn't bring any chap stick," she says. Then she finds some, smears on a slick, thick smile, smacking her lips as we go.

Between the sidewalk and the street, small trees stand in planting boxes, clothed in the tender skin of bark, their leaves changed and dropping, circling in currents on the pavement along with fast-food wrappers and wind-bloated plastic bags.

Padhya squeezes my hand and plants a slimy, medicinal kiss on my cheek. "Fall is so pretty, don't you think?"

I catch a leaf mid-air as it sails on an updraft of warm sewer steam. Red, a fever-sick red, browning in patches, three-pointed like a broken star. The edges curl back, shrinking with death, the underside pale, an eerie green remaining near the yellowed veins. Infection spots the leaf, and the rough mandible marks of some armored worm, an irregular cluster of crusty parasitic eggs.

I let it fall back toward the trash in the gutter. "Best from a distance," I say.

"What isn't?" says Padhya.

She nudges me. Her cheeks are flushed against the breeze, and as I turn to look at her she pulls me closer, touches her lips against mine on her own initiative.

Even as I feel the dumb desire rising, I just want to ignore it, to resist, but she is here, and if taken entirely out of context, in the empty moment, it is almost like it used to be.

We kiss because we always kiss, because it's easier and slightly more pleasant than speaking.

She presses the way she used to press, with strain, that high school desperation. Her hands circle around and her tongue pries at the seal of my lips, eager for a taste of nostalgia.

* * *

Bathroom Cornucopia is nothing but windows, a store made of glass, walls glowing in the dark.

From the street it seems as if the bottles of brightly-colored bath oil and stacks of rainbowed sponges are floating on shelves of air.

Inside, chemical perfume hangs heavy and wet, lavender and glycerin, paper streamer rippling across the ceiling in crepe-crumple waves.

Rubber fish sway in the draft from the ventilation ducts, an ocean medley laying down the ubiquitous shopping soundtrack, keyboards and harp over the mild rumble of surf, the caw of gulls, garbled dolphin speak, the suffocating squeals of humpback whales.

Padhya stands by a display pyramid of lime-green towels. She lifts a few, stacks them back, sighs. She unfolds one, then refolds it, sighs again, this time in my direction.

"I *so* need new towels," she says, "But they sell the

same colors here all year round. Nice for summer, but fall calls for a change."

I stand by a glass counter, baskets of sponges plucked from the deep, gritty, rigid corpses, pore-scouring skeletons.

There are also baskets of hand soaps, greasy little lumps shaped like sea horses, hamburgers, race cars, and, in concession to the season, maple leaves in brown and orange.

Below this are the boxes of non-fogging shower shaving mirrors with folding, adjustable arms and non-slip, suction cup bases. Photos on the sides show smiling, suggestively nude men and women pushing razors across their wet flesh, sex and faces obscured in steam.

The sea gulls in the speakers reach some kind of climax, a cacophony of screeching, the frenzy of fresh carrion and first dives for eyes.

My lower lip is chapped just enough to crack. Split open, it bleeds, and I suck the taste of alkaline tang as I examine bathroom merchandise.

Padhya comes at me with an arm-length squeegee/sponge combination. "I bought one of these for the hall, for our filthy showers. But I think the housekeeper *stole* it."

A woman in a terry cloth Bathroom Cornucopia vest comes over and stands at a convenient distance. "Can I help you find anything today?" she asks.

"We're fine," says Padhya. "Just looking."

The woman swivels on her heels, adjusts a pyramid of bathing cap boxes, the display model manicure/pedicure kit.

Padhya stands at a glass wall lined with glass shelves, glass bottles, glass tubes, balms to moisturize dry skin, to dry oily skin, to achieve an even, bronze tan, to block the sun's deadly UV rays. Beyond the shelves, the darkness outside reflects the interior, a phantom store pierced in spots by streetlights, Padhya's face superimposed over the road.

The gulls cut off suddenly. The waves are back, this time backed by an undertow of whining violins, another instrument that may well be an electric shaver.

Padhya says, "I'm looking for the cucumber-mango revitalizer, but I need the unscented, with vitamin E bubbles, and in a refill bottle, not a dispenser."

I'm fingering a star-shaped bottle of witch hazel and hickory nut bath oil, watching my own eerie reflection standing gigantic in the street.

"Why don't you ask that woman to help?" I say.

"Because I can find it on my own."

The star-shaped bottle slips out of my hand. I catch it before it hits the floor, put it back on the shelf, pick up another bottle, this one shaped like a fragmentation grenade: Cinnamon-apple salve.

"Hey. Look at this. Cinnamon-apple."

"Yeah, I know. It's nice, but I think I'm allergic."

"But cinnamon-apple. Why isn't it apple-cinnamon?"

"Can't you just help me?"

"What are you looking for again?"

"Oh, forget it." She stands, smoothes her dress against her thighs. "Revitalizer. I guess they just don't have it. I'll be at their other store soon, anyway, the bigger one, out west. It's a better store, but I just thought, since I was *here*."

She takes the cinnamon-apple salve from my hand, places it back on a shelf.

"Please try not to break anything, Martin. This is an expensive place."

* * *

We head back to her campus in silence, walking on the cemetery side of the street.

Beyond the wrought iron at our right, lambs and angels dot the rolling terrain of the long-since dead. Headstones ring the slopes along the lagoon, chalky in the dark. Icy shimmer of mausoleum stained glass, the stubs of stone tree trunks severed before their time.

Padhya pulls on her gloves, takes an ear warmer from her purse, slips the black knit band over her forehead and works it under her pony tail in the back.

"I wish I had driven. I should have, it's just so hard to find a spot on the street, and I hate that tiny parking structure. It's dangerous, bums hiding at every corner. Everything will be better once the new one gets built."

"It is cold," I say. "Why don't we just take the bus back?" I point to the frosted Plexiglas bubble of the RTA stop, the huddled commuters standing by the curb, peering off for a first glimpse of their bus.

"The bus," says Padhya. "Are you kidding? No, thanks. Not me. Maybe you didn't hear, but last weekend some woman was raped and murdered on *the bus*."

"I heard," I say, "But that was in California."

"Bad things happen in Ohio, too. You don't think so?"

"No, no, they do."

"All the time. Things that don't make *the news*."

"But… I just meant..."

"I'm not riding the bus, Martin. I had a long talk with my mother about it yesterday. She didn't know I had been using public transportation at all. She had *so many* stories. She promised to reimburse me for cab fare if it ever came to that."

"When had you been using public transportation?"

"Allie and I took the bus down to Tower City and back. Twice. And I've ridden the train, too, out to the airport."

"Alright," I say. "Let's just drop it. We're walking."

The wind picks up again, and I tie the flaps of my cap down over my ears. We come to the entrance to the cemetery, the big electric gates, the gatehouse, the modern section stretching out, marble slabs, flush with the earth, garnished with empty metal vases, raised metal hooks.

Padhya says, "There are presidents buried here, you know. I was thinking of taking a class on it."

"The burial of presidents?"

"On this cemetery, silly. It's an historic site, very famous. They do tours. And there's a class, too, one that fulfills my Arts and Humanities requirement. Everyone says it's fun."

"I'm sure," I say. "I mean, it's a cemetery."

"Don't be *macabre*. It's beautiful in the summer. *Landscaped*, like botanical gardens almost, with swans in the lagoon. People come and picnic. *We* should come and picnic."

"Ok," I say.

"We used to picnic."

"I remember."

"We used to picnic all the time. We had picnics in my parents' basement when it rained. Remember? You were so *sweet* back then, Martin."

We turn with the graveyard wall, head down the hill along the oldest fence, stacked stones, Civil War soldiers on the other side.

She takes my hand in hers, the cold smooth leather of her gloved palm. Twin strands of barbed wire lean inward on metal struts across the fence top.

"And that one time," she says. "You had that tape recorder, that tape of harp music."

"That time was soup," I say. "Soup for a picnic."

"You were always crazy and funny and nice."

"Then what happened?"

"Then it got harder for us to talk."

"Somehow."

Without street lamps, only the passing cars light our path. The wind rushes up the incline, sharpening itself, straight from the lake, straight from Canada. The sidewalk is slick and steep, the panels tilted up by the roots of cemetery trees, concrete coated in shade-thriving moss.

"Yeah," she says. "I hate this hill. Hold my hand, ok?"

"I am holding your hand."

"I know. But don't let go."

* * *

The slope evens as Little Italy begins, a village nestled in the city, a flurry of suspicious boutiques, the Old World charm of second- and third-floor curtains parting, dark, as we pass.

"Elderly women are watching us," says Padhya. "They're probably not fans of my skin color, but I bet they really hate your hat."

"What's so bad about the hat?"

"It's just weird. *You know*. I'm sure the things that embarrass me about it are the reasons you wear it. It represents a certain approach to life, right?"

"I embarrass you?"

"The *hat* does. But, yeah, you do, too. Sometimes. Like that scene at the cafe. You're so resistant to things, like you're so proud of this hick, small-town heritage thing."

"Hick?"

"No, that's how *you* see it, like in your hunting cap you're more *rural* than the rest of us. And it bothers me the way you sometimes think its cool to act like no one else matters."

"Sometimes no one else matters," I say.

"Your hostility toward the world. *That* bothers me. In part because I feel that it's often aimed against me, too, that I'm lumped together with these things about life that disgust you, that make you angry."

"You know you matter to me," I say.

"I think *lots* of things matter to you, Martin," she says. "You just don't deal with all of it so well. Somehow you manage both to wear yourself on your sleeve and to act totally callous and indifferent."

"Immune?"

"Don't do that, don't obsess over the phrasing of things. You always turn meaning around just to find nice words, or ignore meaning altogether."

"This is pretty heavy stuff, Padhya. These are strong allegations."

"I'm not making *allegations*, Martin. And this is important. This is what we need. This is me talking about how I feel, me talking about *us*."

"You've been holding this back for a while."

"You've been avoiding me for a while. We haven't had a chance to get things said."

"I haven't been *avoiding* you."

"Whatever. I'm curious what you and your friends say about me, about us. I hear some of the things Allie and her clique say, but you and your friends, you're all so consciously constructed. I mean, you all probably sit around formulating philosophies, quoting, I don't know, great thinkers."

"My friends are not familiar with great thinkers," I say.

"That's exactly the sort of thing I'd expect you to say. Punky, self-deprecating smartness."

"Padhya, you're sounding like a *therapist*."

"Probably because I spend so much time going over all this with mine. Look, they finally closed that bakery that refused to serve anyone who wasn't white."

She points to a storefront boarded with planks, painted green, white, and red. Next door is an art gallery, its windows draped with marionettes. Melodrama stock types hang like sausages at a meat counter, wolves and damsels, strapping woodsmen and soldiers, witches and suave villains, mustachioed, with top hats.

"Didn't some kid get beat up there, a University student?"

"We had lab together. He was in a concussion for a while. But anyway, it feels good to get some of this off my chest. I've felt awful about us lately, and I don't want to have to feel like that. Are you hungry yet? We should eat around here. It'll be fun. I know a place that's authentic and good, where all the mafia types used to go."

She leads me toward a red door, a restaurant tucked away, small, round porthole windows flickering red through their curtains, uneven chunks of stone rimming the wide sills.

"There was a drive-by here last year," she says. "See the valets? In summer, people wait along the sidewalk here for their cars to be brought around, and I guess it's a pretty easy spot for a hit. Years ago some mafia don got his throat slashed by an assassin posing as a valet, and then last year there was the shooting, about six people were hurt."

"So the mafia types don't go here anymore?"

"They go somewhere farther east."

The door's wide and thickly painted planks are

rounded at the top, fit to plug the cave-arch gap in the building's face. It groans apart from its frame as she pulls, a rush of interior heat against our faces. We step into a waiting room packed with people, walls loaded with crossed armaments, old maps, bouquets of dried peppers and herbs, vaguely ethnic accouterments, weapons of war.

Padhya goes up to the hostess podium, comes back again. "Forty-five minutes," she says. "A private party's bought up the main dining room."

We stand in the stone arch of the doorway to our right, looking in at the rows of tables in the big dining hall. A fire snaps in the hearth, sparks spitting against the screens.

Candelabrum light dusty through the dense wood smoke, the scent of vinegar and garlic, the crowd, trimmed in pearls and fur, glinting cufflinks and heavy rings, gnash their cutlery, slosh their snifters.

A mandolin player strolls between the aisles, his tune all but smothered by the amplified intimacies of the crowd, the roaring whispers, laughter that breaks like choking sobs, full of glistening teeth.

We step back into the waiting room, wedge ourselves into a free spot along the wall, under a double-headed hatchet wrapped in plastic-leaved grape vines.

Across the way, on a wooden pew beneath a rack of pike arms, sits a blonde couple in matching University windbreakers. Padhya waves at them, but they stare past her.

"Forty-five minutes," I say. "You sure it's worth it?"

"It's not such a long wait. Not for a good meal."

She looks at me, then down, chews her thumbnail as she watches the crowd watching each other, examining the busy, clogged walls.

There's a suck of wind as the door opens, and more

University types step inside. She tilts her thumb to the side, still chewing. Something shatters in the party room, laughter.

"So," I say. "Anyway."

The nervous twitter of mandolin strings washes over us, and one of the hostesses comes for the blonde couple, leads them down the hall to one of the back dining rooms.

"Were you saying something?"

"Not really."

"I'm just kind of zoned out."

"I was only trying to make conversation."

"It's really loud in here. I can't hear you if you mumble like that."

"I'm not *mumbling*. Maybe you could hear me better if you looked at me."

"Oh. Ok, so now I'm *looking* at you. Eye contact. Is that better?"

"I didn't mean it like that, Padhya. It'd just be nice to talk."

"It's kind of distracting here, Martin. I'm hungry and my head hurts. Can't we just stand here, can't we *not* engage in some kind of heavy discussion and still be happy together?"

"But wouldn't it be nice to be able to talk about something other than my faults. To be able—"

"You're not saying that. I can't *believe* you. I remember trying really hard to express something very important to me at the coffee house, even rushing a little to fit in as much as I could before you cut me off to dwell on some more of your stupid, selfish angst."

"You mean how angry you were that you skipped your tutoring session to see me?"

"You show up an hour late with some vague story about what the hell you were doing, your eyes nearly swollen shut, your voice all quick like you'd just taken a bunch of *uppers*..."

"You could have resisted the temptation to check your watch every two seconds."

"I'm upset because you're just *passing through,* that I only get to see you for a couple of hours at a time, and that only because one of your friends *ODs*."

The man standing beside her coughs into the collar of his overcoat. The woman with him is rolling a playbill in her hands, studying her nails.

In the other room, the fire pops again, and I can feel the heat right behind my collar. The buzz of conversation has gone still, as if the entire waiting room is holding its breath.

"We're in an awfully public place for this," I say.

"That shouldn't bother you, Martin. None of these people mean anything to you, they don't *matter*, they might not even *exist* in your mind."

"Don't be *absurd*," I say.

"You're one to talk," she says. "Such *mature* headwear."

The group of University kids across the way exchange nudges. The tallest of the guys, in front, cocks his eyebrow at me. His sidekick gives me the thumbs-up.

* * *

I pull off my cap. In my hands it seems unreal, the gaudy hyper-glow of color. I flip the lining forward, tuck the hat inside out, broad plaid swaths of green, thin bands of deep red, a dark, musky tone, like wood decoys, old hounds. I fit it back on my head.

Padhya reaches up, adjusts it. "I didn't know it was reversible," she says.

"Yeah. Good deal, huh?"

"You didn't really make it, did you?"

"No," I say. "I stole it from K-Mart last night. I was drunk."

"I think everyone in this room is watching us."

"Nah. Not the hostesses. And not that woman over there. She got embarrassed, has been pretending to study the trade routes around medieval Sicily since your line about mumbling."

The woman turns, gives me a look like a deer staring into headlights after a car has severed it cleanly into two twitching, kicking pieces of blood-drenched flesh.

"Hi," I say. I raise my fist in greeting.

Padhya checks her watch.

"I hear this place is worth the wait," I say.

She says, "We're not really going to wait forty-five minutes, are we? You're only here for a little while, then you have to go back."

"Right. I think we should make the most of this visit."

"Oh, I'm sorry. Let's just leave. Let's go back to the dorm. We can cook Italian."

* * *

The cathedral's spires nub out in stone thorns.

Blind saints huddle sandal-foot against the cold, clustered together in womb-like recesses, their names chiseled below their soles, all shot full of vowels.

Padhya twines her arm in mine as we walk down the sidewalk, the night sky sullied by the city's ambient electric glow, a slurry, urban street fog.

She kisses me across from the stickball mural, the painted history of the Italian New World, immigrant ships and immigrant faces, the images peeling back or patched in wide whitewashed squares to mask the previous layer of gang tags.

In the mural, men with rolled sleeves toil together, and there is the rustic romanticism of construction scenes, canal mules, lettuce markets.

"I don't think I meant all that," she says. "At least I didn't mean to say it all *there*. You know I'm sorry. And embarrassed. I'll *so* never go back in that place again."

She presses her face against my shoulder as we pass under the railroad bridge, oily dark columns and beams, random structural hardnesses.

Bulk boxes of disposable diapers are spilled across the road, few intact on the divide between the lanes but most ruptured, burst, flapping out white plastic wings. One diaper is caught in the crotch of a steel support. Several have been plastered flat to the pavement by traffic, free edges fluttering like half-killed birds.

On the other side of the bridge, beyond a chain-link fence beaten nearly horizontal, the land slopes up, wild with raggy scrub, some industrial drums, crates, a few slumping tarps of shanty tents, fire pits, one spot still smoldering red far up the rise.

Across the street another scabby mural offers a message about hope and the future, working together for a better society. Obscenities and several giant, stylized cocks have been spray-painted across the scene.

"I need to get money anyway," says Padhya. "I was just going to use my credit card at the restaurant, then have you pay me back in cash, but now I can stop by the ATM."

A long building at the corner of Euclid has a cash machine built into its brick corner. As the wind shrills around, Padhya pulls seven cards from her wallet before she finds the right one, then gives me a look before she types in her code, sheltering the screen with her hand.

"No offense, silly boy, but it's not my money, you know?"

So I look off to Euclid, neon tubes, a man drinking from a bagged bottle, frat boys loading pizzas into their car.

An ambulance streaks past, running with its lights, but silent.

There's a chatter and squeak of shopping cart wheels from around the back of the building where an alley empties out at an angle to the street.

I turn to watch the woman advance. She's muttering to herself, her face twitching, one hand clutching the wiry skeleton of a ceiling fan to her breasts, the other hand rattling the cart, as she pushes toward us.

She bucks her cart against the lip of the elevated platform around the building, leaves it, steps up, waddles over to me.

She's huge, bundled up in dirty fabric, a gap-gummed rot of a face, snot beading from the end of her knobbed, raw-red nose, eyes twitching, wide.

"You," she says, hissing in my face. "You. Boy. You heard them, you *know*."

Padhya pockets her wad of bills, lets her receipt fall to the ground as she grabs my arm, pulls me back, close against her.

There's something caked in the old woman's hair. She cradles the fan's guts, leans down and kisses the cracked glass of the lamp dome.

When she looks up again, her eyes are teary. One sharp tooth protrudes at her quivering upper lip.

She calls me sir now. "Sir," she says, "Excuse me. Excuse me, sir. Please. I am homeless, and I am looking for my baby, my baby girl."

Padhya whispers my name, dragging me slowly back toward the curb, down the step. At the intersection, traffic whines and groans. The woman lurches toward us, wobbling, then stepping back to her cart, dragging it as she comes after us again.

Padhya leads me to the crosswalk, a flashing red hand, and the cart tilts and slams sideways against the ground, spilling its hoarded city jetsam across the strip of grass, the gutter.

Crushed cans and shells of rusty scrap metal, wads of wires, coiled cords, rags, wadded newspaper, rubber arms and heads of baby dolls. The woman drops to her knees, wailing.

Padhya and I make it to the other side of the street. The woman, howling now, screaming incomprehensible phrases, spreads her arms out over her possessions, her form framed under the mechanical, shearing, wedge-shaped wings of the corner's public art.

The giant sculpture spins its silver-gray blades across the air above the woman's fists as she shakes them at me, screaming, "You shit, you fuck, you little fucking shit. You give me back my baby. Give me back my baby. My *baby* . . . "

She stands, lifts up the fan. She pulls back and launches it into the street. A car makes a quick swerve, blasting its horn.

The fan just lies there, blades akimbo, glass broken, wires sprawling.

Padhya keeps holding onto my arm as we walk past the gourmet burger joints and cocktail bars, the faded cardboard displays in the travel agency windows, advertising distant minarets and castles, beaches and forests. Her grip is hurting me.

"That was a little like a nightmare," she says. "Except there weren't any tests involved. No pop quizzes on lab procedures. She was crazy, actually insane."

We walk on, silent, then Padhya sighs. She relaxes her grip, makes a face at me, opens her mouth as if to say something, but waits.

Finally, she says, "Why is it that transients always wear gloves without fingers? I mean, I used to think that was just a caricature, but it's true. Did you see her gloves, fingerless?"

"It is a bit clichéd," I say

"What I don't understand is, fingertips get *cold*. Extremities, they're the first to freeze."

"Maybe there's extra dexterity or something. Is that the right word? That it's easier to grab things, pick things up."

"Feel your way through trash, you mean, looking for, what, *recyclables*? Is that what they do with all that metal they collect? They sell it, right?"

"You could pick up small things," I say. "Coins."

"Right. Or turn the pages of a magazine."

"Button up a coat," I say.

"Did you see that phone booth? Someone's knocked all the glass out of it again."

"Eat," I say. "I mean, maneuver small things into your mouth."

"The phone doesn't work, anyway. I tried to use it once. There's a sticker warning you that all calls are monitored by the police department."

"Strike a match," I say.

"I hate this city," she says.

* * *

Pornography, organized alphabetically along the wall of cigarettes and lottery tickets, forms a slick collage of peeping skin behind the Rite Aid register.

Asia Girl, *Ass Man*, *Bare*, and *Barely Legal*, but our business is at the food aisle, between the dry goods and the freezers, down from the concentrated juice mixes, frozen fiestatas, and pressure-loaded cans of cheese. We select a box of house-brand spaghetti noodles, a jar of generic tomato sauce. Padhya insists on a recognizable name for the carton of Parmesan. The store offers only one variety of green olives, lanced with segments of red pimentos.

Our shopping done, Padhya leads me to the hair-care section, where, above the shelf of lice treatment and dye, above the baggies of baby clips and ponytail holders, she points out the bullet holes left from last week's shooting.

She prods me on until I insert my finger in each of the three, past the ragged, blasted chunk of drywall, into the stone.

She seems satisfied, tells me again the story of who was killed and why, which of her friends got to examine the bodies over at the medical school.

* * *

The sky holds the rose glow of city darkness as we follow diagonals across her campus, a paved, handicap-accessible path around the edges of buildings, an aching cold gusting against us, wind drenched in the gamey, sweetmeat stench of dumpsters.

Spotlights are planted around every decorative sapling, bathing their slim, smooth trunks, and hook-shaped lamps crane from the corners of walls, flooding the brick in patches.

Veins of dried ivy vines lace the stone facades, clotting around the exhaust fans under the rose windows of the University's original chapel, now the smallest of its three gyms.

Scrunch-faced dragon dogs leer down from the roof's rim, dry heaving from their drainpipe mouths. Padhya shapes her face like a mask.

"We should have just waited for the campus shuttle,"

she says. "Not that standing at the corner of Euclid is any safer than this."

She pulls me off the path and we cut across gravel, giving wide berth to a new piece of art, coils inside coils, metal receding into a twisting cave, segmented like a giant worm.

"Someone was raped behind that thing on the night of its unveiling, like an hour after the ceremony. Now every weekend someone climbs inside it and screams and howls, says Satanic things. It's like a megaphone, with an echo effect that alters the voice. They make noises till security comes to chase them away, which, whatever, hardly ever happens."

Like phosphorescent breadcrumbs, our path is laid out in blue emergency bulbs.

* * *

Padhya lives in the fourth of four matching towers, the sixth floor of a girls-only building, rich with the confined scent of toaster pastries and powdered laundry detergent.

We take the elevator up, a plastic tampon applicator in the corner, a set of "HELLO, my name is" stickers stuck all over the doors, the same indecipherable gang tag squiggled across each one.

Dolphins cut from construction paper decorate the doors of her hall, each with pasted-on accessories selected by the R.A., symbols of each student's personality as culled from the University's one-page computer housing survey. There's a dolphin with a rack of test tubes, wearing lab goggles, a dolphin in a hard hat with a roll of blueprints, but for the most part the dolphins just have little construction-paper textbooks under their fins, felt-marker titles distinguishing the, say, Civil Engineering and City Planning dolphin from the Biochemistry and Molecular Biology dolphin.

Padhya's dolphin still wears a stethoscope, but she's drawn an immunology book under its fin on her own.

Allie threw her sociology dolphin away orientation week.

"I have a surprise for you," says Padhya, her hand on the doorknob. "We redecorated."

Inside, the cinder-block wall behind Padhya's desk is coated in glossy magazine photos of men, silhouette cut-outs superimposed over larger, more abstract forms. Whole pages arranged in fans or long, linear spreads, the glisteningly monochrome chests of cologne models, the flaring blonde mane of a top tennis seed, the moody, brooding new European movie star. Bare chests, one ass, quite a few ads for briefs with their truck-like thighs and bulging cotton, a marble bust of some strong-jawed Roman emperor, a well-laundered young golf pro, a few aging newscasters and minor politicians, the next Young Turk or Silicon Valley entrepreneur, a charismatic cult leader still in hiding. Rock singers, rock guitar players, rock drummers, rock bassists, one famous crossover bluegrass/rock fiddler, a rock harmonica player, an entire rock horn section...

Allie's sitting at her desk chair in front of the television, working a crossword puzzle. She leans her head back over her chair, watching us upside down.

"Hi, Martin. Let me just say I have *nothing* to do with all that. This room turns me asexual. And tell her to be careful, Thumper's out of his cage."

Padhya groans. "Ask her how she could let him get out again, Martin."

"Don't let her boss you around, Martin. And don't worry about all those old posters, she just moved them over her bunk."

Allie gestures toward a pair of posters for blandly commendable values, the kind grade schools make their kids peddle for funds, kittens curling together above a rhyming quote about the comfort of love, ribbon-chokered puppies above a platitude on devotion.

These inspiration qualities of household pets are intimately tied to my first memories of sex, Padhya and I trading our dull virginity for a quiet, mutual pain, me taking her from behind while her parents held a party downstairs. She stared at the locked door, expecting a knock, and I, doing my best with her advice to finish fast, stared up at this shaggy pair of dogs, their eyes liquid and black as ink.

"Yeah," I say. "Good you didn't just throw them out, Padhya."

"I will never throw them out," she says.

The shades of the window are closed, and more men are pinned to the drape's drab fabric, a pair of call-in radio show hosts, a media mogul, a motor company CEO, some guy in a suit, pounding his fist against a podium, banners of martial eagles behind him.

"Who's this guy?" I say.

"Some German," says Allie. "It was from one of *my* magazines, some article on the new right. He's making a speech about immigrants. And the handicapped, I think."

"Padhya," I say, "Who is this guy?"

"I don't *know*. But he's got a great chin. Now ask my roommate exactly how she could let her stupid rabbit get out of his cage again."

"She and I aren't speaking," says Allie. "But I'm pretty sure he's in the closet. It's a small room. He'll come out for food eventually."

"Thumper?" says Padhya. "Thumper?"

"Why aren't you two speaking?"

"Thumper? Ask her. She's the one not speaking to me."

Allie sits up again, snorts as a response. She points to a crossword puzzle clue with her pen. "'Of Babylon.' Five letters, ending in E."

"I hope she's aware that if he's in the closet, and if he eats my shoes, then *she'll* be buying me new ones. And that won't be easy on *her* budget."

"Come on," I say. "This room is too small to be fighting, especially clogged with all these men everywhere."

"Don't you turn against me, too, Martin. Are you going to help me find the rabbit or not? And Allie and I aren't *fighting* anymore."

"We're just not speaking," says Allie.

"But why *not*?"

"It's not important now. It's not important to talk about it. *She* knows."

Allie says, "Want some tea, Martin? It's got caffeine."

"Sure," I say.

"And that's a *rad* hat."

"Thanks."

"What brings you up here in the middle of the week, anyway? It's hard to know what's going on now that I'm not in communication with your girlfriend."

"This guy got sick," I say. "It's a kind of complicated story."

I clear off a half-dozen stuffed animals so I can sit down on Padhya's bunk, willing myself to forget their stupid names as I move each one: Droopy, Pie-face, Goldie, Linus...

"Well, good to see you anyway," says Allie. "It's always nice to have a human in the room."

She plugs in the electric tea kettle, gets me a mug from Padhya's bookshelf, some pharmaceutical company propaganda, the chemical structure of a cancer-fighting drug on one side, the drug's logo on the other, some sort of double-headed knight armed with a pair of spiky maces.

"Would you mind telling your mature and faithful girlfriend that her mother called?"

"Gee," says Padhya, stepping out of the closet. "I wonder if my mother called yet today? And I really wish someone would put the Britta back in the fridge for a change."

"Martin, if it's not a hassle, tell your girlfriend that there's no room in the fridge. Not with all those leftovers from her date with *Raul*."

"Fuck you, Allie."

"Hey," I say. "You're speaking again."

"She broke first," says Allie.

"Martin, tell my roommate I hope her rabbit's dead."

* * *

The television is on a commercial, a woman twitching the wings on her panty liner, pouring out a full pitcher of blue-dyed liquid.

Cut to cross section, absorbency in action, the thirst of a cross-weave filament. Cut to women rejoicing, free to enjoy their office work.

Allie's at the other end of the desk, waiting for the whistle to sound. Over her shoulder is the bulletin board where Padhya has pinned multiples of our old formal pictures, the acned brow of prom, her bow-fronted bodice, a maroon cummerbund.

And the carnival photos, King and Queen on our hay-bale throne, me clutching my scepter like a roller coaster handle, her tiara askew, streaks of mascara at the edges of her eyes.

Allie hands me the mug of tea. "Hope you like it," she says. "It's sassafras."

"What are you watching?"

"Couples."

"Ice skating. And tell her to turn it down."

"Figure skating, Martin. And this is the good part. They're about to fall, and he's going to cut her face open with his skate. Look, they'll show it again. Oh, slow motion."

A man in a gold cape spins round and round, a very small woman in a very small gold skirt swinging through the air from the end of his arm, and when he slips, suddenly, his feet slide out, intercepting her there at her arm span's outer circumference, and she flips into the air, a full somersault, then down again on her back. She sits up on the ice as the man regains, stands, still spinning, his own foot outstretched for balance, and this foot hits the woman, catches her full across her face, the gashing shown in slow motion, a cold steel hooking of the flesh, a cape of blood flapping up, then covering.

"Shit," I say, as the cameras cut to the audience, two bundled pairs that must be the couple's parents.

"It's 'The Best Of.' They'll show the tape of the Russian having a heart attack soon. They keep running the teaser for it during the commercials."

"That's brutal," I say.

On the television, the very small woman in the very small gold skirt presses a blood-drenched hand to her face, holding her left eye in its socket with pressure. Her partner's scream makes a little cloud in the air.

Padhya's on her hands and knees, checking under the bed, behind her hope chest.

The rabbit streaks across the floor, into her still-open closet.

Allie either doesn't see or decides to ignore the animal's

dash. She says, "How's the tea? My grandmother mailed it to me. From Ashtabula."

I take a sip, warm and rooty, a bit of licorice, an aftertaste of wood. "Nice," I say. "Earthy."

Padhya says, "There you are, you beastie. Martin, tell my roommate I found her rabbit. Warn her, I'm going to the end of the hall to get the fire extinguisher."

"Don't you *dare*, Padhya. Thumper? Here, boy."

Padhya stands at the door, hand on the knob. Allie crawls into the closet, comes out with the rabbit, a lump of black fur kicking like a frog. She carries him to his cage, a long, screened trunk along the other wall. Thumper scratches at the lid, but Allie works him down through the top hatch.

"There you go, boy. It's ok. It's ok. I won't let that mean witch come near you again. Calm, calm." She strokes the cowering thing. "Martin, tell your girlfriend that she can go to hell."

Padhya pulls pairs of shoes from the closet, dusts off their toes, inspects them in the light.

Allie locks the rabbit cage and sits down again, takes a long, slow drink of tea.

She taps at her crossword puzzle with her pen, reads another clue. "Ten letters: 'Psychological condition. Obsessive/_____.'"

Padhya says, "How about five letters: My roommate. Starts with 'B'"

I say, "How are your shoes, Padhya?"

"Jesus," says Allie.

She twirls her hair with her pen. The television's back on commercials, anti-diarrhea medicine, a man in a meeting, clutching at his gut, contorting in his seat, his face glowing green.

"My shoes are ok," says Padhya. "Tell her we're

going downstairs to cook. Tell her I'm going to fill out an application for a change of roommate."

She picks up our Rite Aid bag, takes a bottle of red wine from behind the mini-fridge at the foot of the bunk beds, a corkscrew from her shelf.

"And tell her I'm keeping this room."

Allie leans back again, winks at me upside down. She hands me her folded magazine, a note written in block letters above the crossword puzzle's grid.

"Tell your girlfriend that, yet again, I refused to acknowledge her empty promises."

I look down at the page in my hand. The letters read: "LEAVE HER."

* * *

We take the stairs down, past the different floors, totem animals cut from construction paper taped to fire doors: Sparrows and mice, sheep, unicorns. At the base of the stairs is a lounge, the dorm's front door, the desk where the Resident Assistants take rotating shifts checking visitors into a log book. There's a big billboard for the posting of hall events and security reports, flyers for women's self-defense, the suicide hotline, and some Star Trek marathon. The next room over is the TV lounge, where a bunch of people in black t-shirts huddle together on the couch, one braiding another's hair as some space drama plays out on the screen, a three-eyed woman caressing a man's cracked, purple face. "Of course I'll still love you," she says. "I'll always love you. I don't care if you're a virus."

Padhya and I take our supplies down another hall to the smallest lounge, the kitchen lounge, across from the only men's bathroom in the building.

This lounge is used for bike storage, too, three long

looping racks crammed with the skeletons of bicycles and their hooks and locks and chains. This lounge is also used as a music lounge, a piano in the far corner, opposite the sink and stove and microwave.

Padhya closes the heavy violet blinds along the outside wall, then walks back to the door, checks to make sure the lock works, clicks it shut again.

I peel back the plastic seal from the top of the wine bottle, holding the cool glass neck. I steady the screw, sink it down into the pulpy flesh of the cork.

The walls were painted by some RAs a few years back, an undersea fantasy. Cartoon waves break along the ceiling. A smiling manta ray wings beside the door. There's a cute squid squirting out purple ink. A buck-toothed, bug-eyed moray eel chases a school of rainbow-striped fish behind banks of dead coral, swaying sea anemone fronds. Two big white-bellied sharks circle above the piano, slit eyes and slit gills, silky curve and upturned razorblade tails.

Padhya arranges the supplies in a neat row along the edge of the counter. Above the fan hood is painted an open treasure chest, some starfish at its side, a bare white human skull.

"*That* was unpleasant."

I pour wine into red plastic Solo cups as Padhya searches through cabinets and drawers for the other things we need, gets out a pot, dishes, forks, a can opener.

"It's against the rules to have a pet in your room, of course. Not that the rules ever mean anything. I spoke to the RA about the rabbit, but she doesn't care. She and Allie are apparently friends. They have some dumb Society and Culture class together. But what I really don't appreciate is the way *you* and Allie gang up against me."

"I had some *tea*," I say. "I wasn't party to any larger conspiracy."

"That whole stupid home-bred Ohio thing of yours. You just sat there watching ice skating and making jokes about me."

"Have a drink," I say, passing her a cup.

"I've been saving this wine for a special occasion. It's supposed to be really good, expensive. My cousin brought it out when he visited from New York."

"Great vineyards, New York, a long tradition of—"

"Shut up, Martin. Just help me cook. Let's try and force this to be, whatever, *passable*."

"Pleasant?"

"I don't know about pleasant."

She puts the water on to boil, salting it with one of those gray-and-white cardboard salt shakers that people take on picnics.

"Padhya," I say. "Listen to us. You don't know about *pleasant*? All we've done today is fight. Fight or find some way to ignore each other."

"Ok, we're bad," she says. "Ok? I *admit* that. We don't seem to really work. Is there more you want me to say?"

"More?"

"You want a for instance? Like, for instance, do you want this to be over? Is that what you mean?"

There are tears building along the rims of her eyes.

The stove's metal coils redden under the pot of murky, gray water.

My wine glass is empty, and as I pour myself a second, she empties hers.

"Do *you* want this to be over?"

"No, no, no. Martin, I want this to be *good*. Maybe that doesn't make sense, but I *love* you."

"Nothing makes sense," I say.

"But do you understand that I really . . . I don't *want* anyone else, Martin."

* * *

Bubbles rise in the water, distracted into activity. Padhya shakes the spaghetti out of the box, snaps the strands above the pot, pieces flying across the stove, into the sink, onto the floor. I bend down and pick up some of them, toss them into the sink. A few unbroken lengths of pasta bristle like spines from the edges of the pot. A piece that lands on the burner chars black, gives off a scent of ash, a hint of smoke. Padhya stands by the curtained windows, her hands over her face.

The water boils over with a hiss against the coils. I turn the heat dial down, put the sauce in the microwave. The console has four different sets of buttons, and I try to type in a setting on each of the four pads, but nothing happens.

The room reeks of brine and the heavy odor of pasta steam. Padhya comes up behind me, hugs me, kissing the back of my neck.

She points to a legend at the bottom of the microwave, combinations of buttons that equal pre-set times for standardized dishes. Keystrokes for popcorn, frozen dinners, leftovers.

"Maybe we're just growing apart," I say.

"We have to keep *trying*," she says. "There's so much to save. It's just that sometimes I think you've abandoned this, given up on *us*."

"Padhya," I say.

"I'm sorry. But you don't call enough. And you're never home, or you don't answer the phone, and the e-mail thing... I feel like I hardly know you these days, and talking has become a chore."

I hit three buttons, and the interior of the microwave lights up. The noise comes, and her arms wrap tight around my waist. The carousel starts its spin.

* * *

My girlfriend stands against me, our fingers intertwined. We kiss, of course, red wine's bitter, metallic tinge on her tongue. I drift deeper into oblivion, undulating fish eyes on the wall above her, blue-green scales, tendrils and tentacles.

I hold my breath, the pasta boiling over, gurgling up a head of froth. Sauce splatters against the door of the microwave, red blossoms dripping thickly down.

We kiss, her eyes closed, the room thick with the scent of hard, dry cheese as it heats, bakes, the oily air of olives swelling with internal steam. Sharks circle along the far wall, scenting blood.

* * *

We pull away to prepare the food, soggy pasta, Padhya peeling a thick skin of blackened Parmesan off the sauce. We mix it in a bowl, leave the dishes in the sink.

She goes upstairs alone to see if Allie has left. I sit on a sofa staring up at the arms of a black octopus, pink suckers running to its hidden beak, the lounge air harsh with salt.

When she comes back, she leads me by the hand. In the elevator up I remember the wine, but she says, "It doesn't matter. Don't go back for it."

In her room she spreads a patterned floral sheet, folded over once, across the floor, arranges two plates next to each other, blue cloth napkins in wooden napkin rings.

"Let's pretend that everything is like it was back then," she says. "Just for a little while, let's pretend that things are the way we want."

"Comfortable?" I say.

We are sitting on the floor together, her hand in my lap, her head on my shoulder. She pulls off my cap, tosses it onto her bed. She musses my hair.

"*That's* the word," she says. "I'm so absolutely *comfortable* with you. Of course there's, whatever, *conflict*, but when two people have been dating as long as we have…"

"Things do change," I say.

"There's never going to be the same level of *passion* as before, that original electric thrill, you know? That just doesn't last. But there is this great, comfortable familiarity."

"I love you, Padhya."

"So you should call more," she says, "Because I love you, too."

* * *

Her skin's tint of copper, her hair black and long, full of tight curls she used to iron, a scent of fruit shampoo, fingertips holding the sides of my face.

She told me she loved me for the first time on a miniature-golf course, after finishing the fifth hole, a raspy windmill, broad blades struggling through their gears.

My ball caught on its way through, jamming up the whole mechanism, making the motor whine and click. The attendant came out from the booth where they rented the clubs, an old man, walking with a cane. He lifted the windmill roof, switched off the engine, tilted the blades back until the ball popped free and rolled of its own accord straight across the green, into the hole.

Padhya took my hand as he hobbled off, leaned in close, her lips on my ear, standing on plastic turf in the middle of the country, speaking in words without meaning...

* * *

As she pulls me inside her, I think of you. That sucking give of memory, the warm drag, this ordeal of keeping the past alive.

Burrowing into my mouth, her tongue still tries to speak. Our teeth hit, scrape, and her mouth stretches open farther, as if she could, snake-like, swallow me whole.

Her fingernails dig into my neck, then release. Her hands spread out across my body, arching, kneading, taking hold.

How are you dealing with this same scene, your own slide into time-worn grooves? Do you find a way to remain remote? Are you thinking of me?

I work a gritty, seed-like piece of Parmesan from my teeth as I thrust into her, face to face, but with her head turned to the side.

Her eyes are shut so tight I think at first that she's in pain, but then she starts urging me on, brushes her thumb across my lips on a back stroke.

She says, "Let's be happy, Martin. Let's just be happy."

She's asleep before I can even work off the condom. I dress, check the phone's ringer switch and dial tone, droning distant. I want to be sure I'll get Eddie's call, that I can leave this place, if only temporarily.

I sit on the edge of her bed and flip through television channels in the dark.

A woman slices a pot roast with a credit card. A soldier tours the nursery ward of an orphanage for refugees. A man jumps, in slow motion, from the roof of a building.

The colors flash against all these glossy photos, these flat and anonymous men. A stuffed toy lies on the floor, a cow in overalls, the name of which I cannot recall.

Maybe sex saved us somewhat, that winter her parents threw the party to celebrate the completion of the corporate fund drive, the groundbreaking for the new wing of the new ward, the winter her father arranged for the child killer from Michigan to be moved down to the hospital, the winter the child killer was strangled by another inmate, the old man who cut up all those nurses down in Texas back in the fifties.

And then it comes to me. The fingers just wear out faster than the rest of the gloves. Somehow, I'm crying. I'm crying, and I can't stop.

* * *

When the call comes, we're both asleep. She's shivering against me, under the comforter, in her socks. My shirt's drenched in sweat.

I wake up at some point in the conversation, manage to tell him the address, sketch some rough directions. She sits up as I put down the phone. She presses her hair back, reaches for her clock.

I put on my shoes, my cap. She steps to her dresser, squeezes some toothpaste onto her toothbrush and walks me to the elevator.

"I guess I didn't realize how tired I was," she says.

"It's ok," I say.

"I'm glad you came up," she says.

"Yeah," I say.

Between her yawns, we exchange a series of ready phrases about the nature, extent, and destiny of our love. She asks for promises. I make some.

I ride down alone, staring at the gang tags on the door of the elevator, the spilled carton of take-out sweet and sour in the corner.

At the desk by the stairs the nightshift RA highlights an entire page in pink, her marker squeaking across the print.

I wait at the curb in blue light, my shoulders up against the wind, another cold Cleveland night. I'm standing by a garbage bin, watching my breath rush away, the taste of baked olives, the pucker of wine.

"This stupid home-bred Ohio thing," I'm thinking, the stuffed animals wedged between the bed frame and the wall.

Somewhere, music blares, but here I can barely make out the beat.

I stare at the garbage bin moored in a steel basket sunk in the concrete, metal ribs rising around it.

I turn to the bin, and I kick it.

I kick and kick, kick again, but the bin doesn't budge. There's not even all that much sound, just my grunting, my breath in hot clouds, my foot feeling broken, like maybe some tiny bone fractured, though even that is a kind of optimism, a kind of bravado, a kind of denial.

I limp to the gutter, slump down. I shut my eyes to trap the tears and to help trick myself into identifying every rumbling, distant sound as Eddie's approaching truck.

* * *

A woman's smothered sob, stereophonic.
A man's grunting, struggled push.

Human sounds in full bass, pounding all four speakers in the truck's cab, the narrator's lines ironic to the point of accusation: "Does this sound like pleasure?"

Eddie is covered in blood, a thick cake of black across his chest, flaky patches on his arms, legs. There's even dried blood across the front of his sock cap, some clots in his goatee.

He rattles an aerosol bottle, hands me a damp rag.

"Industrial strength," he says. "It'll kill the smell *and* get you high. We used to do this stuff when I worked for food service. Some really fruity shit."

"Is that llama blood?"

"Hell, no. Pig's blood. Microwaved. Never put pig's blood in a microwave. Sage advice. But how about we make a deal where you don't ask about my night and I don't ask about yours?

"Not that both stories aren't somewhat apparent. You wear your face like a clock, not to mention the fact that I saw you trying to kill that garbage can before I pulled up."

And the voice over: "You are not listening to the act of sexual intercourse. You are listening to the systematic torture and annihilation of a human soul."

Eddie holds down the bottle's nozzle. A mound of industrial-strength furniture polish foams up like thick shaving cream in his palm.

He hands me the bottle with his other hand, then hoists his hand of yellow-tinted lather in the air for a toast. "Cheers," he says. "To heading home."

"What the hell took you so long?" I say.

"I'm only four hours late," says Eddie. "I'm covered in pig's blood. But the main thing is, we're getting out of here. We'll be back on campus by, what, four?"

"Four-thirty, maybe."

"Which is a good five hours before our classes meet.

Come on, shut up and do some household products."

Eddie holds his hand over his nose, breathes deep.

"This is the sound of much more than physical assault," says the stereo. "You are listening to a crippling of spirit, a defilement of body, a shattering of consciousness."

"There's not even music to this one, Eddie. I don't like it at all. I guess I thought there was going to be some sort of corny Schoolhouse Rock rhyme about rape."

I shake up the bottle, spray a thick hit into the towel, hold it over my face. The smell is sharp, hard on the intake but then sweet, lingering along the back channels of the nostrils like strong candy.

I spray another blob into the towel, hand the bottle back to Eddie. Froth is drying in his goatee.

"You're covered in blood," I say.

We laugh a tangy, yellow laugh.

"Filled with guilt and self-loathing, plagued with nightmares, torn to the core, she will eventually by driven to suicide by the memories of her violation."

"Makes you carefree," says Eddie, taking another hit. There are suds in his voice as he reads the label, "'Citrus-Scented General Anti-Bacterial Disinfectant / Furniture Polish.' Did you catch that slash?"

He hands the bottle to me and I skim over all the words on the back, a series of pictographs near the bottom, two of them featuring stylized skulls.

"There sure are a lot of warnings here," I say, giggling.

"Ignore the small print, give me another whiff."

I spray a glob of yellow foam into Eddie's palm. He takes a series of quick huffs. "Lemonade," he says. "Everything is so infinite."

"It doesn't matter that it had been a date. It doesn't matter that she'd known her attacker for ten years, been close friends, colleagues, co-workers. All that matters is that she said 'No,' that she wanted to stop, that she was taken and used against her will."

"Taken and used?" I say.

"But there's that actual sex sound in the background," he says.

"But it's not sex," I say. "It's rape."

"Yeah, but the point of the whole PSA is that it sounds the same."

"Yoder," I say. "The point of the PSA is that it doesn't sound the same, or that our interpretation of these noises should be significantly tainted by the narrative dub-over. I mean…"

"Her independence ignored, her humanity violently disregarded. Now ask yourself: Does this sound like pleasure?"

Here the woman chimes in with a chorus of "No, no, no, no."

"I get hard every time I hear it," says Eddie. "But you can see why it didn't go over so well with the board of trustees."

Eddie wiggles the nozzle of the bottle up his nose. He twists it, and foam covers his face. He gasps, sending the car swerving into the empty oncoming lanes.

"Shit. It *burns*, man."

I lift the bottle to the towel, take another slow hit.

"This is a real citrus kick," he says, wiping his face on his sleeve, sniffing at it, eyes watering. "What happened to your hat, by the way?"

I pull it off, flipping the outside back in, pushing the shape back, dark plaid to hazard orange. I shove it back on my head, tie the earflaps up at the top.

"That's better," says Eddie. "Jesus, a plaid hat is just *dumb*. Let me have the bottle again. I swear I won't fuck up this time."

"I've heard that one before," I say.

* * *

The high dies fast, leaving me with an empty, ice-cold ache inside my sinuses. Eddie pulls a package of tissues from under his seat, and we each blow blood, thin red strings inside the snot.

The buildings of downtown are shadows inside of shadows, far darker than the canopy of clouds pressing down from above.

We wait for a traffic light to change, the only vehicle in sight. The next five slip red in expectation, swaying like armored glow worms in a wind that shakes the truck, whistling through the seal of the doors, the cracks across the windshield.

We drive forward, stop again. A shape stumbles out of the park at our right, falls, struggles to its feet, falls again, goes still.

"Do I even need to talk about how wrong I was earlier?" says Eddie.

"Wrong about what?"

Our voices seem slower, more somber than usual.

"Thousand Island. Swiss cheese. Wrong about hot dog, roast beef, potato chips, you name it. I mean, cheeseburger, ice cream, vodka tonic. I could keep going on forever. Most of the world seems to be arranged in *reverse* alphabetical order. Except coleslaw. I guess coleslaw works, huh?"

"Coleslaw is one word," I say. "That furniture polish was a drag."

"It'll hit our vision soon," he says. "That's not as much fun, but it's ok."

"Will it impair your ability to drive?"

"Barely. I'll just see big yellow spots everywhere."

"Are we going to die on the drive home?"

"Unlikely," he says.

"Well," I say. "Then make it a quick ride, ok?"

* * *

The concrete ribbons curve up, under, their ramps splitting, merging, the highway heading all ways away, out over the cars in hotel parking lots, the stray, lit rooms of salesmen, darkened discount outlets, an all-night donut shop's flickering pink glow.

Trucks haul their freight toward the city, and a weary gray cross-country bus heads for another in an everlasting string of stations. There's hardly any traffic heading out, though. We are all alone in the passing lane.

Juicy sparks flash in my peripheral vision, and I lean against the cold, rumbling glass of the window, staring out at the distances between places and things, forgetting pieces of myself.

As we leave the city behind, I fall into the wasteland's numb embrace, the sullen, silent fields of Northern Ohio, sheds of scythes and bailing machines, the barns where the cows sleep.

* * *

The high school Nazi gang has spray-painted swastikas on both sides of your car, but Sloan is gone, and you don't feel like sleeping.

"You picked up the phone," you say.

"Our machine's busted. And I knew it was you."

"We need to be in person," you say. "Come over. I'm waiting."

* * *

Your cigarette is all I can see of you, a red point in the night.

I get closer, and you're standing in the gravel lot of Overflow Three, Bear's air rifle broken down over your shoulder.

When you see that it's me coming down the alley behind BioScience, you lock the gun shut, pump it three times, quick, and fire a dart at the No Exit sign.

There's a glass snap as the hypodermic chamber explodes, a nautical ringing, the flat metal sign vibrating back and forth.

In the streetlight's dewy haze, a trail of California Sea Lion tranquilizer glimmers like a fat tear down the sign's face.

"You're late, kiddo."

"I took a shower."

"Wash off the smell of your girlfriend?"

"I've never liked that word, Courtney."

"No names, kiddo. I'm armed."

"You sounded pretty rough on the phone."

"But you, kiddo: *You answered.*"

"Yeah," I say.

"Fall into any familiar patterns lately?" you say.

"Let's just say we didn't break up."

"Sloan says he's thinking about maybe doing some ring shopping. Said it romantic like that: 'I'm thinking about maybe doing some ring shopping, babe.' Like a kind of warning."

"Sorry about your car," I say.

It's behind you, the swastika across its hood a little shaky, but drawn in bold, wide lines.

You pump the rifle again, lift it up, take sight at

the bird feeder hanging from the fire escape of the entomology lab.

The feeder explodes, shards of Plexiglas raining down on the pavement of the alley. The plastic plate-shaped squirrel-guard shatters against the top of the dumpster.

"I kind of like it," you say. "Makes me feel like a road warrior."

"Somebody'll call security. I mean, if you keep shooting things."

"In violence is the beginning of wisdom, kiddo. Haven't you learned anything from me? Haven't you learned anything from my life?"

You pump the rifle again, turn, take a step toward the car, aiming point blank.

The dart cracks against the hood, skipping and splattering up across the windshield, a glistening, thick liquid string.

"Courtney," I say.

You pump again, twice, turn at the waist, like in some cowboy film, aiming from your hip, rifle pointed at my head. The streetlights glint off the dent in the metal on your hood.

"Did they put a swastika on your roof, too?" I say.

"No," you say. You lower the gun. "But that would *rock*, huh?"

* * *

We press forward as the last stars fade, clouds and the purple pre-dawn erasing constellations.

We are nothing more than bodies in space, fleeting, like the red blink of your dashboard's Temperature and Service Engine Soon lights, reassuring in their constancy.

Our breath fogs the windshield. You crack your

window to the cold wind. Stop lights blink solitary, the air carrying the scent of bakeries.

A paperboy peddles past, steering with one hand along a jagged course.

We head east, valleys rolling out around us. I shake a cigarette from your pack, hold it between my lips as we pass the skids of spin outs, a guard rail broken open in gnarl-end gaps, a deer's flank and hind legs at the shoulder, broad streaks of blood across pavement.

I mash the cigarette against the orange-hot coils of the lighter, breathe in until the fire spreads, then take it from my mouth, pass it to yours, watch your neck muscles as you inhale.

A car turns at the gates of the plastic factory, and a pickup rattles past us, snow plow blade fixed to its nose with iron struts, tilted back at attention on its hood.

You flick the headlights up to bright, scouring the road. We are alone, on a bumpy but constant climb. You hand the cigarette back to me, and I take a drag.

They've raised a billboard in the lot of the new Holiday Inn, blank white, lit from the bottom, an 800 number for potential advertisers in small print.

We gather strength from our exhaustion, brace ourselves against the dawn, against the weary harvest that ends with the Amish Kitchen's windows lit like television screens, a genre drama of people in red booths crouching low over hash browns, mopping up the last traces of yolk on their plates.

There is only this, this fleeting, buttery hope, this all-night restaurant on a hill.

* * *

The sleigh bells ring clear and steel as we step through the door, half blind, shielding our eyes, dazed from the sudden, swallowing brightness.

We stand by the metal book rack, the paperback romances and self-help bestsellers, the children's illustrated Bible stories, the true tales of UFO abduction.

The kitchen hisses, flares for an instant from behind its swinging doors. The snapping of hot bacon grease, egg whites bubbling in butter. An old man bites into a dry triangle of toast.

Everything is where it should be, ceiling fans stirring the thick tobacco smoke, silverware bound in rolled napkins, sealed shut with calico-patterned paper tabs.

The waitresses move from one empty table to the next, collecting the menus titled *Nite Owl Specials*, putting out the *Good Morning Sunshine*s.

I stare above the back of the skinny state trooper sitting at the counter and up to the mural, less garish at this hour, workers kneeling to harvest celery, stacking the stalks in wooden crates. A man in a sleeveless undershirt dangles a cigarette from his lips as he pours a stream of golden molten metal into a mold, the veins prominent in his muscular arms. Blainville sinks lead territory markers over the side of his canoe. A Moravian-cozy Schoenbrunn cabin puffs smoke from two chimneys above an aerial view of the Great Serpent Mound. But larger than everything else, gigantic and grotesque, Mad Tony Wayne drives that butt home, dead center between the eyes, the smack and crunch of wood stock against skull. Two faces, contorted, savage, the Indian and the Indian Killer, paroxysms of rage, death, this last bloodletting before settlement, the starch collared taming of the land. The face of autumn, the carnage of change. The dead locked in mute, brute, and futile struggle.

Morning comes for us as it came to the sleepers of Gnadenhutten.

I shudder, and you give the portrait a loose, two-fingered salute, biting your lower lip.

You live in the realization that sometimes the violence of history is our last, best hope.

"Sit anywhere," says the waitress, as if we'd never been here before, and we take one of our usual places, a well-familiar window booth on the west side, farthest from the light to come.

You shuck off your jacket, take the cigarette pack and silver lighter from your pocket, slap them down on the generic placemat.

The waitress comes, leaves us with small brown glasses of ice water. You fish something out of yours, wipe it on your pants leg.

The waitress returns, and I flip over our mugs. She sloshes coffee around them, onto the saucers, fills each mug a little more than halfway to the top, splitting the dregs between us, walking away with an empty pot.

You shake out a pair of cigarettes, hand one to me.

"Nah," I say.

"Inside you is a chain smoker struggling to escape."

"I can't afford it," I say.

"It's been proven to cause cancer, kiddo."

"Ok, ok, I'll take one."

"First one's free."

The flint scrapes hard, forming its sharp feather of fire. You hold out Kim's lighter, let me get a start from the flame, cup your hands to light your own.

Our ashtray is full of other people's leavings, scrumpled butts, burnt black, spongy filters cored arterial yellow. This is how truth comes through in mornings, offering an autopsy of someone else's late-night trauma, a butt bent double by a factory layoff, a secret affair's faint traces of lipstick pink.

"I wonder if Bear's dead," you say.

I try to inhale, the cigarette scorching down my throat, into my lungs. I cough for a minute or so, then try again, this harsh fuel scrape of smoke.

I say, "You know what Eddie called it, that California sea lion stuff? 'The refresh that pauses.' Isn't that a good one?"

You don't respond. You study the menu, holding it close, flipping it over, flipping it over again. You're in a sweater I haven't seen before, baggy, a deep sepia.

"Nice sweater," I say.

"You like it? It's irregular. One sleeve's a few inches longer than the other."

"Cool."

"Five bucks."

"A bargain."

"It was a gift. From my aunt. Last Christmas."

"You haven't talked with her again, have you?"

"No. I don't think she'll call back for a while. Although Sloan said he saw her at Niles' new Super Walmart last week. She's already shopping for baby clothes."

A pickup pulls in at the gravel lot of the feed store across the road. A man gets out in a yellow rain slicker, takes a mini-cooler from the back of his truck and carries it to the door, which he unlocks.

He turns on the light inside, and I watch his silhouette as he flips over the CLOSED sign hanging in the window.

The waitress comes and takes our orders, slashing shorthand across her blue-and-white pad. She doesn't make eye contact with us at all.

Someone starts wheezing at the other end of the restaurant, holds his throat with both hands. He slaps at his own back, then tries to stand, falls to his knees beside his booth.

The state trooper stands and folds his napkin. He walks over, squats down behind the guy, wraps his arms around him, and, with a thrust, dislodges some caught chunk of food.

The trooper walks back to his place at the counter, takes out his wallet, counts out money for the check. He leaves a two dollar tip under the edge of his plate, steps over to the register.

"I still hate those guys," you say. "I can't help it. The hats are what I hate most."

A waitress hands a towel to the man who was choking. He wipes his face, shakes hands with the trooper in front of the pie case.

The trooper adjusts his flat-brimmed hat on his head, then steps out the door.

"Did anyone notice what just happened?" I say.

You shrug. "It's early," you say. "I've seen people choke worse than that before. One time I was here with Tegan and this old, fat woman started gagging and choking, really turning blue. Somebody tried Heimlich, but it didn't work. An ambulance came."

I take another drag, not even trying to inhale this time, then tap my cigarette on the rim of the ashtray, let the gray drop off from the finished end.

"You're getting it down," you say. "The next one only costs a quarter."

A horse-drawn buggy heads down the highway, a stuttery shadow, its orange hazard triangle flashing briefly with reflected light.

The sky is a dim violet, fog in the distance, heavy

with the fragrant hint of rain. Thunderheads maneuver like troop formations across the sky.

"Everybody thought she was dead," you say, "But they did something, the paramedics, and she started breathing, coughing up blood, vomit, everything, sitting over there with her back against the pie case."

A man comes through the door of the restaurant, takes off his coat, one of those big black herding trench coats, the kind with a little button-down cape below the collar. He steps back into the alcove and shakes off the rain, the strip of bells slapping. He steps into the restaurant again, wipes his boots on the mat. He walks over and takes the booth directly behind you, hanging the coat on the rack. You glare up at it, squinting, turning your cigarette between your fingers.

"Are you listening to me, kiddo?"

"I hear you," I say. "My ears are in perfect working order."

The man behind you blows his nose, clears his throat. The waitress leaves him two squat glasses of water. The rain falls softly outside.

The waitress pours his coffee, comes and gives us refills. I stare past the window's smudged, fatty pane to the construction site of the new Holiday Inn, the bare metal skeleton, wires draped like flayed flesh from the cross beams.

The blank billboard blocks out the sky, and I wonder how long it will be before people start dumping trash into the swimming pool pit.

You say, "You know what Kim would say about all this. She'd say, 'Life is a chronic, clinical illness, and recognition of the condition is the first step toward a cure.'"

"What does she *mean* by that, anyway?" I say. "What's *clinical*? How are we supposed to understand the word *cure*?"

You say, "That's what things do when they don't *kill*."

"That's a good one," I say. "Point for you."

"See, ideally, we can be both really jaded and happy at the same time, kiddo. Life can be ok if only because we're so familiar with the bad shit that we're immune."

"Immune."

"And we echo each other. You'd prefer *used to it*, kiddo?"

"Familiarity plus comfort equals love."

"Yeah."

"Numb."

"Sure."

"Vegetables and water."

"Right," you say. "To tell the truth, I don't even listen anymore. Each phrase just seems naturally better than the last. What did I say with the word *happiness* in it?"

"Yeah," I say.

"You know, kiddo, Kim Reese had an uncle who made her suck him off when he came to visit. From the ages of, like, three to ten, when her mother walked in on them."

"I didn't know," I say.

"Yeah, but what does it *change*? It's one of those facts I continually suppress. It doesn't fit into any kind of worldview for me. It sure doesn't generate sympathy, or empathy, any kind of understanding or ability to *relate*. It's not *useful*. It's entirely inconsequential to my conception of her character. Girls get fucked over, that's just the way it is."

"Y.M.C.A. booklet number 27," I say.

"Exactly. And then there's number 28, 'Killing the young in her belly.' That's Patchen, too. And I know that line by heart."

* * *

The waitress brings us our plates, a glass syrup bottle, and a bowl of gold butter pats. I unroll my silverware, scrape a crust of something off one of the tongs of my fork.

You take a forceful final drag, then grind your cigarette into the ashtray. It gives off a lingering column of smoke before it is done.

I mimic the move, scraping the butt over the bottom of the tray, pushing away the ashes, revealing the shine of the polished glass underneath.

"You notice we're not asking each other about anything," I say.

"The King and Queen are dead, kiddo. Long live the King and Queen."

"Have we reached some place where talking isn't necessary anymore?"

"We're just on a delay, like the way dreams take a few days to catch up with you when you travel, the lag of psyche, geography."

I shake salt over a massive omelet, its slick, folded flesh oozing soft cheese and mushroom juice from the seam.

The bells above the door ring, and there is the slow folding of a newspaper, the whisper of someone letting out their smoke, the cracking of eggs against a skillet's iron lip.

"It *was* summer," you say. "But there was an icy draft from the air conditioner, and we couldn't turn it down, some car Sloan borrowed special for the occasion, not the bakery van, just some car. I've never seen it any other time.

"We *were* coming from the pool. My aunt had gotten Sloan this stupid summer job teaching little kids not to be afraid of floating.

"There was nothing on the radio. It was broken, too, though Sloan kept trying, fiddling the whole way, hitting those scan buttons, cursing to himself.

"And I didn't pray. That's just dumb, pointless. I mean, I didn't want to be there, but it's not like there was somewhere else I *did* want to be."

* * *

Autumn. You push your plate away, untouched, light another cigarette.

I stab my omelet a few times, watch it leak its fluids across the plate.

I put my fork down, and pick a small, segmented leg out of my hash browns, a series of thorn-like growths along its tibia.

You pass your cigarette to me, then light another for yourself.

"There were protesters," you say. "This is the part I never talk about, not even in poems, some older women, some kids, but mostly just men, men in those awful short-sleeve polo shirts.

"The colors of Easter eggs, cheap pastel golfing colors. Men in pink short-sleeve polo shirts. Men in green short-sleeve polo shirts. Men in yellow short-sleeve polo shirts. There were even men in argyle print.

"And I know, I know, it's fucking Dayton. All the men wear pink polo shirts. But it bugged me at the time.

"And the signs, right? The easy ones were the ones that had been printed, the professional ones, big photographs of medical procedures, glossy blood clots...

"But then there were the homemade ones, magic marker on poster board.

"And, Martin, just the thought of someone making

their daughter sit at the kitchen table, forcing her to practice drawing ruptured fetuses…

"Sloan said something bright about ignoring it all, which I tried really hard to take as an indication that he cared.

"But the way they say it, it sounds like a song, you know? The bit about killing a beating heart, that's catchy. Kind of makes you want to dance."

"I've never heard the whole story," I say.

"That's an apocryphal story, at least," you say. "Much more important than a conventional, linear narrative. Sometimes I think about myself in the past tense, kiddo.

"I know I'm not saying this very well, but that's what scares me the most."

A pink stain of sky seeps through the clouds. You brush a curl behind your ears. Colors can be distinguished now, mellowed by night, this slow patter of rain.

The scumbling of autumn: Red and yellow and brown leaves pasted over the dreary windshields of the diagonally parked cars.

The seasons draw us another dawn, and we sit in a booth, waiting for our food to get cold.

We practice well-tested patience.

* * *

"Sloan and I started dating this one night, spring break, junior year. I met him at some show, not Weak Chin, another band, out of Akron, who had Sloan subbing on the bass, and, well, like I said, it was spring break, in Niles, and there was a keg.

"The band was ok, just this one guy and a drum machine and Sloan. Is it still a band if it's only one guy?"

"A one-man band," I say. "One man can be a band but not a mob."

"And an army. But how about a gang? What if there's only one high school Nazi?"

"Are you kidding?" I say.

"Anyway. Niles, keg, spring break, etc. You know what I mean. In that light, he looked pretty good, like the best thing I'd ever seen."

"He's got a good face, Sloan."

"His chin's ok. His ears are kind of fucked."

"Yeah," I say. "And he's got that Adam's apple."

"I used to think that was so cute."

You smile, then let your face drop back into shape. You rake your thumb across your lower lip, take another hard pull on your cigarette.

"Then the next winter was the big snow," you say. "And right after that, in the first real week of thaw, when everything was going soft and wet and gray, my mother went and did her thing.

"Sloan was over, had spent the night, which Mom didn't care about, but which we had to keep secret from my grandparents.

"I remember, I guess, hearing something outside, so I looked out the window and the whole farm was crawling with state troopers. Everywhere I looked there was one of those stupid, flat-brimmed hats.

"I panicked, made Sloan flush whatever grass he had. He said something brilliant about whether or not he should hide in the closet. I grabbed him, held him like a shield as I went out into the hall.

"Pigs *everywhere*. Cops, troopers, some guys in honest–to-God *trench coats*. And nobody bothering to explain anything to me. This one was like—a trooper—he was like, 'Put on a brave face, sweetie.'

"Patchen again: 'Clipping my chin with his gloved fist.'

"I was so angry. What can you say to cops? Sloan

standing there against the wall, scared—amazed, I think, that none of the troopers were hassling him, didn't give a damn that he existed, didn't even look at him.

"He had this half-smile on his face, like suddenly he was invisible, surrounded by pigs, thinking in his dull way how lucky he was.

"But I was freaked out. I was pissed, terrified. Like being caught in a dream, that trapped frustration.

"I said, 'I live here, officer. Let me into the kitchen,' then forced my way in," you say. "Kiddo. I mean, we have *so much* blood inside our bodies.

"I can't really go on right now, but are you starting to see how it all fits together? As my new legal guardian, my aunt decided I should move in with my soon-to-be rock star boyfriend. She gave us fifty bucks, some groceries, that fern.

"Then I got pregnant."

You pull your plate toward you, pour some maple syrup over your congealing cornmeal mush, moving in concentric circles, pouring and pouring till, with a thin string, the syrup goes dry.

You push your plate away again, light a new cigarette off the one you're smoking, then finish that one off, grind it out in the ashtray with all those butts and dust, that salt-and-pepper ash, the square-cornered cellophane top off someone else's pack.

You pick up the ashtray and dump it out over your mush, take your fork and mix it all together, mush and syrup and butts and ash.

"Like that," you say. "Just like that."

My cigarette has burned down to the filter, singeing my thumb. I drop the butt into my ice water, stir it up with the handle of my spoon.

The rain turns steady, falling in sheets, an ambient

roar as it washes over the restaurant's roof. The sun is gone. The sun will be gone for months.

Only a slight change of light indicates the new day. Sunrise means nothing in autumn, just a creeping dimness.

You do not cry, but your hand shakes as you smoke.

There is a certain tremulous retaking of self in the way you hold your cigarette, like a weapon, on guard, in front of your face.

We drink coffee as the rain falls, cold and constant, heavy against everything it hits.

We drink more coffee, and you stare at me, a flicker of what might be invitation in your eyes.

* * *

I turn to the mural.

A couple of truckers sit at the counter, talking about mileage and load, but above them, there is an order to the fixed forms.

This place existed before either of us, farther back than grade school trivia, the vaguely recognizable names of pioneers and politicians, the crude likenesses on the wall.

Beyond all that, before creatures with two or four or six legs, in the earliest swirls of the protein-drenched primordial sea, there was this sense.

The planet trapped in its measured spin, rotating always away from light, away from warmth, consuming itself through these dumb, destructive seasons.

Above the hallway to the restrooms, Christopher Gist pens another evening's candle-lit entry, that great journal of early Ohio, another book I've never read.

But how does that antiquated diary compare to all this? I mean, weed out the passing slang, the *thous* and *kiddos* of time, and are our recent affairs really a manifestation of something new, or are we just filling in a fragment of some broader story?

"Love on a terminal moraine," I say.

You tap your coffee mug against mine, force a flicker of a smile.

"I think maybe it's farther south, though," I say. "The moraine. I guess I'm not sure if there really are prairies up around Cleveland."

"Doesn't matter," you say. "We've found an appropriate title. Now we just have to write ourselves an ending."

Your hand rests on your pack of cigarettes. My hand rests on yours. Under the table, ours knees brush against each other, hold the touch.

"What do you *want* to happen next, Courtney?" I say.

You look away, squinting toward the kitchen doors, the pie case, the cash register. You pull your knee away, draw back your hand.

"I think our waitress is lost," you say.

"Don't get metaphysical, Courtney. We're just here for breakfast."

"I want the bill. I want to keep moving. I want to get in the car and drive down out of this place, to play one real, actual, good song on the stereo, to open the windows to the rain."

"And then?"

"Then I want to take a shower, and I want to go to class. I want to doodle in the margins of my notebook as some tenured pedophile farts out a lecture on Sherwood Anderson."

"Yeah?"

"Fuck our lives, kiddo. But there is nothing else."

* * *

The man with the hook carries a piece of black plastic tarp over his head, his hook pierced through its edge. The bells ring as he comes in, and he stands there on the mat, grabs the door handle with his hook. Wet tarp dangling, he shakes the door back and forth, jangling the bells. He has a flannel shirt bundled under his arm.

"Maggie," he says. "I need a hand over here."

A man in a black wool watch cap stands and pantomimes sawing off one of his own with a butter knife. There's some laughter from over in the man with the hook's usual section.

The younger waitress comes through the swinging doors of the kitchen. She gives both men hard looks, wipes her hands on her apron, down her thighs.

"What's all the fuss about?" she says.

The man puts his boot down on the tarp, rips it off his hook. He walks over to the counter, where he places the bundled shirt, holding the middle steady as he starts to unwrap whatever's inside.

"Whoa," says the waitress. "No way. Get that thing out of here."

Something wiggles in the shirt, lets out a quick, high-pitched chirp.

"There's ordinances against rodents. It's illegal in eating establishments. The official people take that very seriously."

"Got its little front paw chopped off," says the man with the hook. "And none of the people who come here are official people."

"I'm not kidding," says the waitress. "No joke. That animal could have rabies."

"So could *I*," he says. "It got caught in one of those damn traps everyone's buying."

He lifts up a small gray squirrel, letting it gnaw on his hook, teeth grinding against the metal. The waitress shakes her head, but she's smiling, her hand on the man's hip.

"Oh, cutie. Is he ok?"

"What a pair we make, huh?"

"Will he live?" she says.

"For now. He's already made it. It's not a lingering illness, losing a hand."

The squirrel sinks its teeth into the flesh webbing of the man's one good palm. Blood squirts, and the man with the hook winces, laughs.

"That a boy," he says. "*Now* you're learning. Maggie, you want to patch me up?"

The waitress has a towel in her hand, but she's just watching the squirrel. It cranes its neck, head darting back and forth, tiny black eyes taking in the scene.

The waitress says, "Well, since he's hurt and all... I guess we got some warm milk and fried corn mush back there. How's that sound, cutie?"

"Sounds good," he says. "But the kid's hungry, too. Why not get him some sausage?"

The man with the hook sees us in our booth. He walks over, moving slow, letting the squirrel gets a sense of the surroundings, sound, smell, image.

"A fine morning to you two," he says. "It seems we're in need of..."

He pauses to suck blood from his good hand.

"An analgesic?" you say.

"A *name*," he says. "What's the good word today, Courtney?"

"I'm leaning toward *clenched*," you say. "With *briquette* in the silver medal position."

"Briquette," he says. "I like that one. From a grill?"

"Compressed coal dust used for fuel. Despite everything, it keeps burning."

"Makes a good name, huh?"

You pick out an irregularly large chunk of cold potatoes from my plate, hold it out to the squirrel. It sniffs, grabs at it, catching it between paw and raw stump.

The squirrel holds the potato for a second, then drops it to the floor. With my knife, I peel back a long, limp line of omelet, double it over, hand it to you.

You offer this to the squirrel and, draping it over the good paw, it takes a few nibbling bites. It looks up again, lets the omelet sliver drop to the floor. The squirrel just stares at you.

"At first I had him in a box," says the man with the hook. "But he scratched around, still bleeding a little. I figured he was going to hurt himself, so I wrapped him like this instead."

"He's scared," you say.

"I get that all the time," says the man with the hook. "He just doesn't know me yet."

The waitress comes over with a first-aid kit and a tray of assorted foods, a bowl of jam, nuts, a biscuit, a corner from a frosted cake, some sausage links. She sets the tray down on the table, opens the first-aid kit, taking out some sterile gauze, a tape dispenser, a pair of miniature scissors.

"Are you going to rehabilitate him?" she says. "Reintroduce him into the wild, like that one lady does with the raptors?"

"He's teaching him to eat meat," you say. "That's a start."

"You don't think living with me is wild enough?" he says, pulling her against him with his hook. She struggles, pushing her hands against his chest, pressing her waist against his. He growls, bites at her ear. They kiss, with plenty of tongue, the squirrel held up, just out of range.

She takes the tray and the first-aid kit and the man with the hook and his wounded squirrel back across the restaurant, down the hall to the bathrooms, to the Employees Only door.

Our waitress leaves the check at the end of our table. She is shaking her head, but she says nothing, doesn't even bother to offer us any more coffee.

Your chin is propped in your hands. You look up, studying the ceiling fan, sighing softly, the dry hum and till as the blades spin.

"That guy's life always seems ok," I say, eating a piece of walnut from the squirrel's tray.

You say, "All the good men are amputees."

"Thanks."

"You have nothing to worry about, kiddo. You're in line for your surgery. Any day now."

Hail begins to fall, a clatter across the cars of the parking lot, a machine gun drumming against the roof. One of the waitresses cusses. One of the truckers from the counter crosses to the front windows, staring out at the storm, the frozen rocks hurling themselves out of the sky.

"Our cue," you say. "Let's go, kiddo."

* * *

Fringe silenced by the ice's din, you shrug into your jacket in the room between doors, flyers for lost pets stuck to the windows with masking tape.

Crayon drawings, sketched by a child's hand, a spotted brown-and-black pup and a rougher, more cartoonish cat's face, sharp-toothed smile, eyes slit like split oranges.

Taillights smear red across the wet glass.

I tie my earflaps under my chin, lower my cap's brim till I can see plaid. The hail comes down with a sound like a garbage disposal grinding away an engagement ring, and you turn from the sad-ringed puppy-dog eyes, push the door open with your boot.

We step out into the full fury of the season, this excessive descent, this gravelly onslaught, clouds churning crushed ice, pelting stones down to the pavement. We step out into beaten color, leaves battered down, bare branches quivering, black.

The biggest stones shatter on impact, the smaller pellets skip in crazy ricochets, a racket of marbles poured out, bouncing, ice against metal, a constant ping and clink and pound. Hoods are dented, paint scratched, goods damaged. Hailstones gather at the shoulder like salt, rap and tatter against the red shingles of the restaurant roof, the rooster-shaped wrought iron weathervane, fake, welded in place, unmoving even in a gale.

You squint into the jagged assault, impervious, unfazed. You raise up your face, spread out your suede-fringed arms.

You dare autumn to overcome you.

And for the most part there is no pain. With a quick sting, an ice shard bullets the back of my hand, leaves a bleeding nick.

But the bruise is always worse than the broken skin.

Your cheek is cut, a thin incision across that strong bone below your left eye.

With a shift in the tone of sound, a hushing, the hail turns back to rain, and for an instant I think you are crying, liquid on concrete, soft across the valleys of trees, the tarps of the construction site.

And the gems begin to melt on the muddy strip where the parking lot peters into grass.

And the highway traffic plows on, sixteen-wheelers sluicing rainwater off of asphalt.

A man in a baseball cap and an old Browns jacket steps out of the feed store, flicking up his collar as he walks to his truck. He runs his hand across the hood, puts his fingers in the new dimples and scars.

The clouds charge across the sky.

Big, wet blotches splatter against my face.

Someone at the restaurant's door whistles in relief.

You stand beside your car, running your fingertips across notches, minor lacerations, kneeling down beside the passenger door, tracing the dark arms of the spray-paint swastika.

The rain picks up, harder. Drenched and shivering, we sit in your car. You sort through the shoebox full of cassettes, struggle with the car's starter, teasing the engine till it rolls.

You push in the lighter, shove a tape into the deck. Your face is flecked with blood.

Autumn, and you sigh, breathing past words.

You peel a half-rotten leaf off your jeans, flick it toward the back seat.

The taste of your tar still in my mouth, I lean toward you, take your face in my hands, wipe a watery red streak from your cheek.

You kiss the inside of my wrist, lower your head, lean into me. I kiss your hair where it grows out darkest, at the roots.

We hold each other here, rain roaring down, a curtain pouring, smoke-colored, over the windshield.

You pull away when the lighter pops out, ready, hot. You drag a cigarette from your pack with your teeth, breathe, force the fire to catch, burn.

You wipe your eyes as you drag, hard.

The slick grind of a tape in rewind, spinning back

in search of some perfect phrase. You kick the lever for the parking break and it releases us with a jolt. We roll backwards.

I put my hand on your thigh, and you grin through new tears. You look back to guide us, knock the gearshift so we slide forward. You put you hand over mine, squeeze it.

You squint over at me, lift up your hand, clip my chin with your fist. "Put on a brave face, kiddo," you say. You punch the play button, but we're at a lull between songs, this grainy pulse of recorded silence.

Autumn.

And we drive, away, from here.

SPENCER DEW is the author of the short story collection *Songs of Insurgency,* the critical study *Learning for Revolution: the Work of Kathy Acker,* and the chapbook *Mont-Saint-Michel and Chartres.* Dew is staff book reviewer for *decomP* magazine and a regular reviewer for *Rain Taxi Review of Books.*

CPSIA information can be obtained at www.ICGtesting.com
Printed in the USA
BVOW08s0847311213

340590BV00003B/65/P